In From the Cold

by

Susan Payne

In From the Cold

Cover Art by *The Wild Rose Press, Inc.*

The Wild Rose Press, Inc.
PO Box 708
Adams Basin, NY 14410-0708
Visit us at www.thewildrosepress.com

Publishing History
First Edition, 2021
Trade Paperback ISBN 978-1-5092-3748-7
Digital ISBN 978-1-5092-3749-4

Published in the United States of America

"Katarina, my love, we have discussed this and agreed Alaska is not a place for you. This trading post is not a place for you. Your place is with your father wherever that may be. St. Petersburg sounds like a grand place to me, and you should return to the life you were born to have."

Sobs shook her shoulders, and he looked over to the man he hoped would help him say the right things to drive Katarina back to Russia. She would never believe Matthew had changed his mind about loving her. Glancing across the room, Matthew could see the bear of a man surreptitiously wipe a tear from his cheek and realized there would be no more help from that quarter. It would be up to him to convince her to go home.

"Listen, you know about my early life and I tell you truthfully I would do anything, give-up anything, to spend a little more time with my pa. He died suddenly without any of us being able to tell him a proper goodbye, to thank him for all he gave up for us, to promise him we would work hard and be grateful for what the good Lord provided. I envy you your father. He may be fit and hearty now, but things change, and you still have the time to spend with him doing all those wonderful things he keeps talking about." He pushed her away from his body so he could stare into her eyes. "You know I love you, but that won't go away. You have the chance I never had to spend time with your father. Take it, grasp it to your heart, hold on for as long as you can."

Dedication

For my daughters who spend their time as my beta readers and my husband who understands when I argue with my invisible people.

Northwest Coast off Canada—Summer 1874

CHAPTER ONE

Matthew blew his warm breath into his cupped hands, trying to find relief for what he feared would lead to the loss of fingers. Others, huddled around the small fire burning in a metal kettle onboard the ship, were all doing the same. All in the same boat, his younger brother Simon would have joked. He missed Simon. Hell, he missed them all, but it had been time, more than time, for him to make something of himself.

Living at home and helping his older brother Luke run the ranch seemed like the right choice, but that was when he was a teen. A decade later and the need to break out of the family bonds and make his own way, find his own destiny, became too strong to deny.

Hell, who was he fooling? He'd probably be right back in Nebraska on the ranch his parents left to their sons if Luke hadn't brought home an unexpected bride. His six siblings had mixed feelings about Luke's wife, but within a few days everyone had one thought about her—she was perfect. A good cook, smart. Not just book smart, although she was that too, but common-sense smart. Everyone loved her—including him, although not in the same way the others had. To be honest with himself, he fell in love with the blonde-haired beauty before Luke did.

Trying to ignore the draw she had on his heart had

1

driven him half-mad. Matthew finally realized he needed to put some space between the two of them or his emotions would tear the family apart. Pit brother against brother, and that wouldn't have been fair to any of them. Lorelei would have probably left if only to end the strife, and then all of them would be brokenhearted in their own way. It hadn't taken long for her to become very important to each of them and her heart had been so empty there had been plenty of room for them all. The family she assured them she had always wanted.

So that's the reason he was freezing his tail off onboard a ship taking him to Sitka in the Alaskan Territory. The place where dreams still had a chance of coming true and nightmares were said to be waiting. Although no one dwelled on that part. No one mentioned the unending cold, the unending light followed by the unending night, the lack of people once you got there, or the blisters bursting what skin was left on your hands after picking in the rock-hard dirt all day.

These were just some of the stories they entertained themselves with around the fire kettle. He wasn't sure if they were friendly warnings, or if they were trying to frighten the weakhearted away from the goldfields, or if they were the truth. All he knew was that every one of those men with a horror story about Alaska was heading right back there after getting their grubstake put together again.

They were all a pretty rough-looking bunch after several days onboard without proper means for bathing. His hands brushed back his wind-blown hair and then over the dark beard covering most of his face. He had always been clean-shaven growing up, and it felt odd to feel the bush growing where tanned skin had always been. His bright blue eyes were the same. He saw them reflected in the small piece of mirror above the basin he used to brush his teeth.

As he tried to get closer to the heat, pushing through those who had been there long enough, he thought back to what the man behind the sale's counter in San Francisco had told him. Matthew had learned it was the best store to get what was needed by miners going to Alaska. As he looked over the shelves, he heard a commotion between two German men trying to make themselves clear to the salesclerk.

"I'm not sure what you fellas want." The clerk began ticking each item off, counting them on his fingers. "Ya got yer pick and shovel, a sluicing pan, work gloves, boots, extra wool socks, long johns, a lantern and can of oil for it, a canvass to wrap it all up in, and remember, I said it could be used as a tent if'n you don't find any other quarters."

The two men gestured with all four hands trying to explain what they wanted again.

Putting down the sluicing pan he was looking at, Matthew approached the men and in broken German asked them what else they felt they needed then interpreted for the clerk. "They want a map. Something to show them where the gold can be found."

The clerk looked at all three of them as if they were daft. "Fellas, if'n I had such a thing, do you think I'd be here behind this counter? I'd be a rich man just sellin' the things. Sorry, no maps of anything. Although maybe once you get to Sitka, they may know whose claim is payin' off. Then again maybe not since most miners are real quiet about such things. Only the assayer knows for sure, and he ain't supposed to let on if there's a strike or not."

Matthew related the bad news to the patiently waiting Germans, and they took out several coins to pay for their purchases. Talking to one another about how much they still had to travel on, they left the store heading toward the docks.

There were others in the store, but Matthew hoped the clerk would have a minute more to advise him. "Is it really better to buy all this here and carry it all that way or buy it once you get up there?"

"I'm not saying this just to sell ya things cuz I git paid the same workin' here either way. But if you wait, I know it costs a heck of a lot more up there, and sometimes they run out of things. Usually have to wait for another shipment which can be months apart depending on what it is you need."

"Even things like that pick and shovel?"

"Especially things like that. Miners break 'em on the frozen ground or against rock, and then they're pretty much done for. I mean they can scratch it out of the ground, and I heard of men doing so, but for getting anything worth their while, they need the right tools."

"Sounds like you should have a store up there."

"The boss tried it, but he came back a broken man. Too much need, he said. Hated to tell miners who spent everything they owned to git there that they still needed to pay for essentials, like food. There ain't even free wood for heat. Everything has a cost, and it's expected to be paid in gold. Plenty of thievin' and con games going on, too." He scratched under one arm. "Probably shoulda warned them two others about the maps for sale up there in the wild. Men sayin' they know where gold is, but are too old or tired to mine it themselves.

They sell them things, and these greenhorns go off into the wilderness. Lucky if they make it back to civilization cuz most of them maps aren't ever real past the town borders."

"I hope you're telling them you didn't have any will warn them enough to know they're no real ones. Otherwise, I thank you for the information."

The lanky man gazed at him with a knowing smile. "All that and it isn't keepin' you from goin', is it? I'm glad I never caught the fever…"

"I don't have gold fever. I have wanderlust as our two German friends would have called it. My folks were pioneers and their folks before them. I left the family ranch to make my way in the world, and if that means I find gold, too, then all the better. My six brothers seem content with their lives, but I wanted more, I guess, and what better place than this wild country open for investigating and seeing."

"You make it sound like an adventure."

"To me, it will be. I hear there are mountains and lakes and streams and tall trees never cut before. Coming from a flat land like Nebraska, it sounds like an adventure. Maybe I'll even draw up one of those maps of the area—a real map so folks won't get lost."

"Sounds like you'll need a lot of provisions for doing all that adventurin'. How about a real tent with ropes and stakes, although sometimes the ground's too frozen to set them. Called permafrost. If'n that happens, tie it off to anything strong enough to hold it. The winds can get blowin' something fierce, so try to be in a hollow or behind a windbreak."

He grinned at the man saying, "You should write a book with all these suggestions and thoughts. Probably

5

sell like hotcakes to us greenhorns heading to a country we never even heard of much before this."

"We got some right over there." Pointing to both hardcover and paperback books of various thicknesses. "Some in Russian with funny squiggling words. No maps though, like I says."

As he added things to the growing pile, Matthew hoped he was going to be able to carry everything the clerk thought necessary for the trip—the adventure of a lifetime.

Matthew rolled with the ship, which rolled with the waves, trying not to lean too much and fall over like some of the others had. He made his way to the burning kettle set up on blocks. A small pile of cut wood was next to it, but a sailor was stationed there to feed it in slowly. The man warned them all that there was a limited amount of wood, and when it was gone, it was gone. There would be no more heat above deck. The only heat below deck was from the fires that ran the steam-powered engines, but the putrid odor from bilge water and musty, damp cloth drove most of the travelers above board. With those engines going full blast, they would make Sitka in six days as long as they didn't run into ice floes or storms.

The sleeping was rough, using hammocks below decks without blankets or pillows. You furnish your own or go without. Meals were served twice a day with plenty of coffee and little meat. Fish soup, fish stew, salted fish—as long as you liked fish, salmon to be precise, you were fine. Sourdough bread finished out the meals. He looked forward to getting to dry land, a nice restaurant in Sitka, and ordering a big Nebraskan steak.

CHAPTER TWO

The harbor at Sitka was well established as he eagerly watched the many ships loading and unloading goods and equipment. Several of the men he had travelled with were already lining up to disembark, wanting to be the first to get to the goldfields just outside of town. Matthew wasn't mean enough to remind them there had been others arriving for the past twenty years all looking for their own piece of land. Being first off the ship wasn't going to give them more of a chance at finding a good claim.

Gazing over the horizon, he remembered what his new friend, Tedero, who he met onboard, said about the town and when the Americans took over from the Russians. The Russian-American Company had warehouses full of items. Tea kettles, copper wire, cloth, and trousers that had been stockpiled for the locals' and immigrants' needs. All had been shipped back to San Francisco, leaving the warehouses empty and men without jobs. Those first few years under the American flag took a busy port city from over a thousand people plus native tribal members to less than three hundred. Tedero explained the Russians, fearing their way of life was ending, sold up and went home. Americans who came to fill those places found they were not cut out for the bleak weather and near-vacant landscape. Admitting it was a beautiful country with large lakes, flowing rivers, green trees, and high mountains, those men didn't think they could make a living there or bring their families. They went home after a couple of years leaving dozens of buildings boarded up and empty.

Matthew heard his friend call out, "Hey, dat is good Kentucky whiskey, so no more jostling of dat crate. You hear me?"

Men were already lifting barrels, crates, and sacks from the hold with some items dripping bilge water and smelling like dead fish. Matthew turned his face upwind to find some relief from the odor. He heard his name called and returned to his friend's side.

"Did you want help getting this to your wagons, Tedero? I have nothing pulling me anywhere else, you know, so I can give you a hand if you need me." The large Russian with his dark hair and beard heavily streaked with gray was still admonishing the men raising the ropes on pulleys.

"I thought I would hire a man to go with me from the warehouse district, but I trust you, and that is priceless in a land such as this. You will get a free guide to take you to the area rich with gold unlike the overworked claims within the town's limits along the river. It is beautiful country out there free of people and clutter. Only the earth, wind, and water…"

Chuckling, he asked, "You're scaring me, Tedero. Are you trying to lure me into helping because no one else will go with you to this trading post of yours?"

"*Nyet, nyet*, my friend. I like you, and we have more to teach one another. I want to hear more of this Nebraska, and I will teach you about Alaska. I have been here many years and have travelled much of it, but

Sitka, Sitka is my home base. Most Russian's still in this land live in Sitka. It used to be called New Archangel, did you know? Many things changed once Russia no longer owned this land—not all to the bad, but it changed."

"I want to learn about the history of this place and agree you'd be a good teacher. It's an adventure I can't turn down and one I know I'll enjoy."

Readying himself to work, he asked, "What do I do now?"

The rest of the morning was spent getting Tedero's supplies out of the hold and down the gangplank to a waiting wagon. Wiping the sweat from his brow, Matthew said, "I thought you said we move provisions to the trading post by canoe then overland till we reach a river. How do we do that with all of this? It will take a big canoe."

"First, we use a barge or boat until it gets too narrow, then the canoes, then portage, then the canoes again. I do it many times a year, no worry." The large man shrugged and waved to the driver to climb into the box.

"I can drive a wagon, Tedero, if that's any use to you. You'll have to show me how to paddle a canoe, since we don't really use those in Nebraska. I'll learn a new skill right off."

"Come, my friend, I will teach you a new skill first. I will show you how we Russian's drink vodka. You know vodka?"

He knew from talk aboard ship that whiskey was expensive in the territory, but no talk of the cost for other alcohol. Matthew wasn't really a drinker, so he didn't worry about the cost or availability. He drank a beer in town on a hot July day once in a while, but that was the extent of it. "No, don't think I do. Is it your national drink or something? Any good?"

"Very, very good, my friend. I will show you as soon as I make sure my provisions make it to the warehouse safely. Then we find vodka and beautiful ladies, no? A beautiful woman always makes a good end to a trip." He clapped his hand on Matthew's shoulder, laughing heartily as he led him toward a row of large plain barn-type buildings.

The next morning, while holding his head to keep it from falling off his shoulders, Matthew complained, "Oh, Tedero, that was not kind of you. My head feels like it will explode. I learned my lesson about drinking too much whiskey back in Whitewater Rapids when I was sixteen. Never been that foolish again—until last night. Your Russian vodka is too strong for this greenhorn."

"Greenhorn? What is this greenhorn?"

"It means someone who's so new to something he doesn't know how to behave or what to do. Easterners would come out to homestead and get driven out the first year not knowing how to even begin to farm or ranch. They just see the cheap land and chance to work for themselves not realizing how much work and common sense is required."

"Ah-h-h, I see. A *cheechako*. But you will soon know all you need to know to survive here in the inside passage."

Sotto-voiced Matthew added, "If I survive the first lesson."

A big hand clapped him on his shoulder which still ached from the previous day, although Matthew was used to throwing heavy bags of grain onto his shoulders and calves during branding. He was finding new muscles he didn't know he had and a head that felt too big for his hat.

"See? That is why I like you. You understand there are penalties for not learning the lessons. You might be feeling better if you had taken one of the women to your bed as I suggested. You like women, don't you?"

He shook his head at having to explain his motives. "Yes, I like women just fine, but I'm here due to a woman, and, I guess, I'm not a man who can think of one woman and bed another."

Tedero became quiet as he nodded in commiseration. "I would like to say I know how to rid yourself of such a problem, but I cannot. I, too, am haunted by thoughts of the woman I loved. Her early passing was one reason I came to this land to wipe out all memories of her, but I could never forget—here deep inside." He thumped his barrel chest then stood and gathered up his outside gear. "Come, we will eat big breakfast and then find more men to take us upriver."

Matthew wasn't interested in eating, not with the way his head and stomach felt, but he hoped an Alaskan breakfast included strong black coffee. Thankfully, it did.

They spent the rest of the day talking to friends of Tedero and a few strangers possibly going their way towards the summits. Placer mines were tapped out closer to town, and most miners were planning on going further inland, even as far away as White Pass. Tedero's trading post was about half that far. They finally ended at a long-time friend's home, a large two-storied shipboard-sided house with several windows and a wide front door. It had been painted a bright red at one time but was weathered now. Still, it appeared well tended in all other ways with candles and lamps shining from most of the windows.

As they entered the low doorway, Tedero bent his head and then grabbed a small child and began pretending to eat its belly while the child wiggled in throes of giggles. Soon others were jumping up and down asking for their turn with the burly visitor.

Matthew couldn't help the smile that crossed his face because he could remember his father doing something similar with his younger brothers. The large man who seemed to be the children's father looked on in amusement as well. When each child had been summarily devoured, they were sent off excited and laughing.

"Welcome, my friend. I see you've brought a new friend?" Their host, looking like a copy of Tedero, didn't seem surprised by Matthew standing in his home.

"Matthew," Tedero placed his hand on Matthew's shoulder and brought him forward, "meet my oldest and dearest friend in Sitka, Peter Kashevaroff, and his beautiful wife, Natolla. Peter's family has been here for generations and can truly claim to be an Alaskan. All those little ones are his children and grandchildren. His youngest daughter, Ophem, just got married at fifteen, so by next year, God willing, there will be more."

Waving them toward the fireplace, their host said loudly as if speaking to an army, "Come in and take off your coats. Natolla always has the fire roaring in here. Says it is to keep the children warm, but she doesn't fool me. I feel her cold feet in my bed each night." He laughed at his daring, but the look the couple shared told Matthew there was no malice in the man's words.

Matthew hung his outerwear on large pegs by the door along with several others and wondered how many people actually lived here. It made his family of eight seem small. He moved to the wooden stools near the fire where Peter was already pouring out small glasses of vodka. Matthew's stomach put up an argument, but he thought it would be impolite to refuse his host's hospitality.

He mimicked the other two men as they raised their glasses in the air in a toast and chorused, "*Boodeem zdarovye!*" Matthew's voice a few beats after the other two.

Tedero translated as he lowered his glass to be refilled, "To our health!" Matthew knew where this was leading. Last night began the same way but he thought, in for a penny in for a pound.

With glasses raised again, the two large Russian's said, "*Za nashoodroozhboo!*" Matthew chimed in a tad behind the others while trying to keep the tears caused by the strong drink from running down his cheeks.

"To our friendship," Tedero translated. The drink fest was interrupted by Natolla bringing over a wooden tray with thick, sliced brown bread and a creamy pungent cheese. Matthew followed Tedero's lead and spread the cheese on the bread and took a large bite. Not having eaten since the night before, Matthew was ready for food, and drinking on an empty stomach was already causing his head to spin. Thankfully, both the bread and cheese were very good. The rich rye bread was similar to what the German's made back home, but the cheese was unfamiliar to him.

"Tell Natolla for me that this is very good cheese," Matthew said quietly to Tedero.

"It is a favorite from the steppes made from mare's milk. We import it by way of the ships that still arrive here from Russia."

Holding up his second piece of bread and cheese, he nodded, thanking his hostess who smiled widely showing even white teeth.

"*Da, da,*" she said, returning to the large pot hanging over the fire.

The men sat down on the three-legged stools and chewed their food before beginning their talk. "Peter, I need a couple of good men to take Matthew and me to the mouth of the river. You know of someone in town? Everyone I know is off seal hunting since a large herd was spotted north up the coast."

"*Da*, I heard the same, but I do know of some Haida who have several *umiaks* that are trustworthy. How much are you taking with you this trip?" Peter reached for a pipe leaning against a lamp on the table and took a couple of puffs, bringing the tobacco embers back to life. He handed it toward Tedero who took a few puffs who then handed it toward Matthew. He didn't want to offend anyone, but the thought of tobacco on his already squeamish stomach might make things get too out of hand. At his hesitancy, Tedero simply handed the pipe back to his friend.

"That sounds as if it will work. How much will it cost per boat?" Matthew recognized when the businessman showed up and leaned in realizing the negotiations had already begun.

"One troy pound per boat. You will pay for their meals? Maybe a bottle of whiskey?" It seemed Tedero may have met his match. Matthew had seen Tedero in action twice now. Once in San Francisco harbor when he negotiated the shipping cost of his freight and the second onboard ship negotiating to get his supplies off-boarded first.

"I will pay for food and a bottle of vodka, no whiskey." Tedero's voice was firm.

"For each crew member?" Peter held his friend's stare.

"*Da*, for each adult crew member. I not pay for children learning their trade."

Peter put out his hand, and Tedero clasped and shook it. "This is good. We drink to our bargain. What the hell, we drink to everything." Both Russians laughed as if it were all a big joke, and Peter refilled the glasses—all three of them.

"You stay for supper, da? I know Natolla will take offense if you leave without tasting her *ukha* which she has been cooking over that fire for hours."

Tedero answered for them. "*Da*, I was hoping for an invitation. The aroma alone was worth the visit." He smiled at his own teasing, and Natolla giggled like a schoolgirl while adding more spices to the simmering pot.

The men were fed where they sat. More brown bread, a bowl of pickled pieces of raw fish, which Matthew recognized as herring, and a steaming bowl of soup thick with vegetables, some of which he also recognized. Leeks and potatoes, he knew, some cabbage and carrots but that's where his knowledge ended. He stirred the food and blew across it, disturbing the surface and allowing it to cool. His two companions didn't wait and were spooning the hot soup into their mouths, dipping the brown bread into the broth and eating that also. Matthew sipped tentatively and then took a bigger spoonful. He knew it had a fish base from eating mainly fish soups onboard ship for more than a week, but Natolla made it much more palatable. In fact, he was beginning to appreciate the difference between the two and agreed with Tedero that Natolla was a very good cook.

A young boy brought over some scored crackers, and each man broke some off and placing a piece of the pickled herring on top, popped it into their mouths chewing with relish, even Matthew. He wished his brothers could see him now, see him on this Alaskan adventure.

He was dizzy, but not feeling the pounding any longer. Perhaps he was becoming used to this vodka. The men sat back replete while young girls removed the empty bowls and spoons.

"Dat was good. *Nostrovia*, Natolla," Tedero said, leaning back against the wall behind him. He scratched his chin through his thick gray beard saying, "You are one lucky man, Peter, one hell of a lucky man."

Peter smiled broadly, "I know, my friend, I know."

"Well, we will have an early start tomorrow. Send the Haida to my warehouse where I will meet them. Hopefully, we can be on our way soon," Tedero said, as he went to stand.

"*Ha nocowoki*?" Peter asked, then said to Matthew, "One for the road?" Lifting up the almost empty bottle of vodka, shook it invitingly.

Matthew glanced toward Tedero to see how he should answer that. So far, his large Russian friend hadn't turned down a chance for a drink.

Tedero sat back down. "*Da*, just the one. Already I'm not sure my young friend will find our way home, and I can't remember it either." This brought a roar of laughter from both Russians and a smile from Matthew. As he drank one last glassful, he could only hope Tedero was joking because Matthew knew he didn't know where in the town he was at the moment.

CHAPTER THREE

The morning was crisply cold, but six men wearing various animal pelts, their dark hair bare, and intelligent dark eyes inquisitive of the new cheechako, met them outside the warehouse. Thankfully, the Haida spoke Russian since Tedero admitted his *Xaat Kill* was weak. Matthew watched as the men began making a pile of items Tedero pointed to as being needed for their trip. After it was all together, the lead spokesperson for the group told Tedero something, who then replied, and it seemed more negotiations were being made. Finally, the conversation and the hand gesturing came to a stop, and the two men shook hands. Tedero looked very pleased with himself as they left the six Haida to their work in the warehouse.

"Come, we will eat now while they decide the best way to pack the *umiaks* to keep them balanced."

Matthew followed his friend to the same restaurant as they had eaten at the previous morning when Matthew only had coffee. He hoped it served what he was beginning to think of as regular food. He was about ready for that dreamed-of steak.

Tedero ordered for both of them, calling it across the heads of the many men already seated. Matthew took the time to watch the various customers, noting the new arrivals with their dark jean trousers and unscuffed, waterproofed boots to those with battered hats, gloves with trouser knees rubbed through by rough rock, and the kind of expression often seen at funerals. Alive but wondering why.

A man brought them both a plate of flapjacks, sausages, and eggs with what looked like tiny, black pearls on top. Matthew's stomach rumbled with hunger, but he didn't pick up his fork as Tedero did. Waiting until the server poured the coffee and moved away, he asked, "What's on the eggs? It looks strange."

"Caviar. Fish roe, you know? It is good."

Matthew began scraping off the offensive fish eggs.

Tedero stopped shoveling his food into his mouth. "You not have fish in Nebraska?"

"Yeah, but we use the roe as bait for other fish, not to eat ourselves. Bass love roe."

Using his fork, Tedero took the slippery roe and transferred it to his plate. "Well, you people in Nebraska are missing out, feeding such glorious food to the fish. No wonder you are so small and weak."

A smile showed through the other man's beard, his blue eyes sparkling, and Matthew knew he was being used as a means of humor. He picked up one fish egg and slid it between his lips hoping he wasn't making too big of a mistake. It burst on his tongue, and the salty fishy taste filled his mouth. Not as bad as he first thought, and eaten along with something like the egg, it was probably quite good. Giving in to his friend's questioning look, he said, "I might try it again sometime."

"Like when you haven't drunk a third of a bottle of vodka?" The glint of humor was even more obvious now.

Breaking the yoke of his egg, Matthew answered with a smile, "Yeah, like then."

Matthew's shoulders were screaming for relief, but he kept the rhythm of the paddles, his gaze on the horizon, hoping someone would call a halt to the trip and make camp for the night. As it was summer, the daylight seemed ever present, so he had no means of figuring out the time. It seemed like forever since they left the island and entered the inside passage. Since then, he had seen thousands of islands, all sizes, many uninhabitable by humans.

They were on the last leg of the journey, Tedero assured him. The Russian had talked the Haida into portaging with them, and the next stop would be the trading post on the bank of this tributary. It might have been an easier trip if they hadn't been paddling upstream against the currents, hadn't been shoved into the three *umiaks* like sardines, hadn't eaten dried fish dipped in seal oil for every meal, and hadn't had to sleep at night slumped against the supplies. Otherwise, it had been a great adventure.

He had seen his first whale, although Tedero said it was a young male and not very large, a dolphin, although he couldn't see the difference between that and the Dall porpoise they had spotted earlier. A Steller sea lion sunning itself in the freezing wind, and sea otters by the hundreds playing around most of the islands they passed. It seemed those were the best since the Haidas got very excited and pointed and talked between themselves. He thought they planned on hunting on their return trip to Sitka.

The men began paddling faster as if sensing the end of their journey. And then he thought he smelled wood smoke. Did that mean they were almost there? That they would sleep on land again? Have a hot meal, warm fire, and actually feel like men and not some sort of water creature who only went on land to do their business.

Tedero called from one of the other *umiaks*, "See, I tell you it is the most beautiful spot in all Alaska. We will be home soon now."

Matthew forgot about his sore muscles and plunged his oar into the water as deeply and as smoothly as the other two men in his *umiak*. The Haida added another man, so there were three to move each boat forward. He had his doubts about the smallish vessels, but after a few hours felt as comfortable maneuvering one around the shallow sections by the islands and submerged tree stumps and branches as he did cutting out a calf from the herd. Maybe comfortable wasn't quite the right word, since his gloves had been soaked in a matter of minutes with the wind blowing the spray from his paddle back onto him. The Haida did much better with their fish skin and grass-padded mittens and seal fur mukluks.

Now another adventure. Living at a trading post along the route to the goldfields and popular Dead Horse Trail. He will see miners before and after their experience, maybe have time to hear their stories. Looking around he could see why there were no maps to speak of. The inside passage was a myriad of bushy islands and tributaries emptying into the ocean further on. The depths around the islands changed with the seasons, so if he were to make a map like he planned, it would begin on land from the trading post.

They pulled into dugout sections along the bank so

21

the boats could be tied to tree trunks not far away. There was a smaller version of the *umiaks* they arrived in and a couple of canoes all upside down pulled high up the bank. The barking of dogs got louder and more hysterical than when they were paddling closer. It looked like there was enough to run a dog team. The men were met by two people waddling out of the cabin bundled to their noses, smiling, and chattering in Haida and Russian. Matthew hoped they knew some English as well, or he might get lonely with only Tedero to talk with and the occasional English-speaking miner or trapper.

Tedero waved him closer. "Matthew, this is Kimalu and his wife, Suu. They are my two employees. Suu cooks and cleans some for me. Kimalu is a good tanner and trapper. I let him make the deals with the other trappers because he can tell a good fur from a great fur. I never cheat my customers, so they return again and again. I make it up by charging the fur buyer more for them. He pays. He knows a good deal when he sees one, too. He usually only wants the best, so it is easy to charge more.

Putting his hand out to Suu first and then Kimalu, Matthew smiled. "It's good to meet you folks. Maybe tonight you can tell me a little about your life here in Alaska. I'm eager to learn all I can, and it seems like you might be a good teacher." Kimalu nodded, smiling, then bent to begin taking items to the store.

Once the *umiaks* were unloaded, Suu fed them sourdough bread with hunks of seared meat topped with seal oil. It had a slightly fishy taste, or maybe that was the oil. Either way, it was hot, filling, and Matthew was getting used to seal oil. The fire was banked as everyone found a place on the floor to sleep, some bundling together. Matthew was surprised that Tedero bedded down with Kimalu and his wife after taking off his outwear. The Haidas removed everything unashamedly before sliding between the furs making up the sleeping beds.

Tedero offered to slide closer to Suu who was between the two men, but Matthew shook his head trying to figure out the proper protocol of sleeping this way. Tedero yawned saying, "Then pull down some of those furs and make your own bed, but it is warmer to sleep with others."

After a little rustling of furs, soft snores filled the silence, and Matthew stared into the still-glowing embers, thinking Alaska was the strangest place he had ever found himself—and find himself was what he planned on doing.

In the morning, the Haidas ate fish and more bread before getting their bottle of vodka and food for their trip back to Sitka. Matthew followed Kimalu, who thankfully did speak English, as he fed the sled dogs frozen salmon, helped him split the logs piled for fuel, refilled lanterns with the pungent whale oil, and followed a trap line that was set for snowshoe hare, pika, which he learned was a large rodent, fox and porcupine.

They returned as the sky darkened, and he watched as a hare was skinned and stretched, which he knew how to do already and a muskrat which he was not used to skinning. He wasn't sure if Suu hadn't fed him one last night but wasn't going to ask. Best just be thankful for a hot meal and no more tough, dried fish for a while.

When it became too cold to work outside, everyone

had their own work inside. Suu wove grasses to use as insulation in mittens and boots, Kimalu strung animal gut forming snowshoes, Tedero carefully cut patterns into fine fur, and Matthew took up his lifelong hobby of carving animals from interesting pieces of wood. Whether he helped on the trap line or just cut kindling, he was always on the lookout for new woods to use. His carving implements went with him everywhere, and he had spent some time onboard ship carving animals and giving them to shipmates to send home to their children. It had always been something he did to relax or think. He had made larger pieces like the cradle for Luke and Lorelei's baby. The last thing he made before leaving for Alaska.

After the fire had been banked and everyone ready for sleep, a loud cracking sound woke Matthew from his doze. "What is that sound? It's as if the whole cabin is shifting, trying to break apart."

"No, not break apart, but it is getting colder," Kimalu answered, while Tedero snored next to him un-phased by the loud popping. "The sap, the moisture in the wood, is freezing, causing new cracks in the beams. Will not hurt the building but will make for a noisy night."

"I should say so. Almost like a rifle going off." He pulled the covers up over his ears to keep both the sound and cold out.

CHAPTER FOUR

"Matthew, it has been good times with you here, better than in long time. We play cards or chess each night, you help stock shelves, and help make up new, what you call it? Inventory ledger. You learn how to measure and grade gold. All this in but a few weeks. Is this the adventure you dreamed about?" Tedero took a draw of the pipe between his lips and stared at the fire, his feet cozily warm in the woven grass socks Suu made for them both.

"I wake up each morning raring to go, so it must mean I'm still interested in all of this. I've enjoyed the trappers who've come through and the mushers. Can't say I understand how a pack of dogs can pull a full sled of furs and provisions, but they do. I'm still fascinated by it all, so I guess I'm still having my Alaskan adventure."

"Dat is good. I once felt like dat every day too, but not so much now."

Matthew wasn't sure what his friend was telling him. "Is there something I can help you with to get the excitement of Alaska or the trading post back into your spirit? I think I could take care of things here if you want to try your hand at mining for a while."

He placed the pipe onto the hearth. "I'm glad to hear you say dat, my friend. I do want you to take care of the business, make sure Kimalu and Suu always have a home to come back to after they go seal hunting in the north. They are loyal friends, but this is not their life. Trapping, hunting seal and walrus—that is their real life, their real reason to live."

"Kimalu told me when he explained the totem pole of his family outside. It was fascinating seeing the eagle, bear, everything having a meaning and telling a story. Our Nebraska Indians have their history as well, but it is already getting lost with the changes. I agree, he wouldn't want to be held down in one place forever, but it's good of them to help you out when you need to travel back for supplies."

Still staring at the glow from the firebox, Tedero continued, "I want to travel back—back to Russia, to a little town in Siberia where I was born, where I was married, where I belong."

"How long do you plan to visit? Would you be staying long?"

"I fear I will be staying quite a while. I plan to go home to die."

Matthew stared at his friend, hoping it was a form of a joke, something Russians said for a laugh. From his friend's expression, he could tell it wasn't, and Matthew's heart had a little bump before continuing beating regularly again. "Why now? You were the one telling me how wonderful Alaska had been to you, how you loved the people here, the land itself…"

"My Anna is buried there, and I want dat for me, too. You are a good man. You treat Kimalu and Suu like proper man and wife. Many look down on these people who welcomed us when we first came here. You will be fair with the men who have learned that here is where they will be treated fairly."

"Tedero, I appreciate what you're doing here. But giving me something that took you years to build." Matthew shook his head in denial. "I'd buy it from you in a minute, but you know I don't have squat."

"Okay. We play for trading post." He pulled out the ever-present deck of well-worn cards and began shuffling them on the table. "We will draw as you say. High card wins all."

Matthew shook his head. "I have nothing of equal value to bet with even if I thought you were serious."

"Matthew, I am serious. I have lump." His eyes filled with tears as he looked up meeting Matthew's steady gaze. "It is a bad lump and meeting you has given me the chance to go home before…I want to lie one last time next to my Anna."

Without any other words passing between them, Matthew walked over and pulled a card from the deck splayed out on the marred wood table. Flipping it over, he stared at the queen of diamonds.

Tedero laughed. "A very good card, my friend." Then pulled one for himself flipping it on top of the spread deck. A nine. Tedero laughed harder, slapping his knee as he did so. "My friend, you should see your face. You are now the proprietor of this fine trading post, and you look like someone punched you in the gut."

"I can't take this from you. Let me make payments or something until it gets paid off. We can decide on an amount, and I can send it to you and…"

The man's big hand came over Matthew's smaller one. "No, my friend. I have thought about this all the way from San Francisco. I tried to find a buyer in America, and there were no good men that wanted to come here. I looked onboard ship for someone to help me with it, and you found me. You are the right man—a good man for this trading post. Do not try to pay me. A dead man has no need of money."

Matthew shook his head, sad at learning of his friend's impending end. "When?" He cleared his throat. "When will you be leaving here? Do you have another winter?"

"No, my friend, I was told not to plan on seeing the end of the year. I will head back to Sitka and find passage back home to Anna. I promised her I would return to her, and I think I better do so soon, or she will be angry that I did not make it."

"I can't say I won't miss you and your advice, even if it was sometimes hard to listen to. I came to Alaska to find myself, make my own way, and you showed me we all follow someone's footprints. I am grateful to be following in yours."

"When I am in Sitka, I can sign all the papers. I will explain things to Kimalu and Suu. They will understand my need to leave so soon again. I will leave you with the best wishes for your future. This is but one step for you. There is much more waiting for you in your life, and this is but that first step."

He was surprised to find Suu and Kimalu packing the next morning. "Are you leaving, too? Didn't Tedero make it plain you are more than welcome to stay. I need the help as much as he did."

Tedero answered for them. "They were planning on leaving to hunt seal and walrus further north. They come and go throughout the year. They will be back in a few weeks once they kill enough meat. Kimalu promised to bring back a caribou, so there will be plenty of fresh meat as well."

Kimalu added, "This way, Tedero doesn't need to make the trip back to Sitka alone. We will go and make sure he is able to travel by ship as he wants. His spirit needs to be at rest at home. Alaska had his life, but now he must meet his maker."

"I'll take care of everything. Do I do anything special with the dogs?"

"We will take all the dogs but Aitii. She is the oldest and will stay and keep you company. Chase off the bears." Tedero said lightheartedly, thinking it great fun to try to scare his friend.

Matthew pushed aside the man's teasing. "I'm used to bears and coyotes and mountain lions, but I'll appreciate Aitii's company anyway."

He stood by the bank until the two vessels were out of sight before walking back to the trading post which now belonged to him. The beginning of another part of his Alaskan adventure.

Staring up at the open beams, Matthew wondered how far Tedero got before making camp. The large Russian had left with a few tears falling, Matthew's included, knowing he would never see the man again. Knowing why he would never see the man again. Life has so many turns and twists it made him worry about Lorelei and his brothers. Wondering if her baby was all right, if the younger boys were doing well in school, if everyone was hale and healthy.

He never thought about how much he would miss being near his family. When Luke brought Lorelei home, a stranger who soon made her way into all their hearts, it seemed a natural extension to the family. Even Luke, who had always been the most stalwart, wasn't immune to his wife's perfection. She was beautiful, maternal, and loving. And Matthew lost his heart to his sister-in-law immediately. It was at that point when he knew there would be no chance for the two of them to be together as he wanted. She let him down as easily as she could but left him no hope that she would change her mind.

She had helped him realize that he was not so much in love with her as he was in love with the idea of finding a place to belong, someone special to belong with. He had always let Luke, as the oldest, make the decisions for the ranch and family. There was nothing Matthew would have done differently or that he disagreed with, as he followed Luke's lead. But there was only a year different in their ages, and Luke was married and expecting a child, while Matthew felt as if he were treading water.

He sent a prayer of thanks to Lorelei for helping him understand what he felt before he caused a break in the family he loved with all his being. Looking back, he saw how badly things could have gone and how well they did go due to his sister-in-law's kindness to a member of her adopted family. He rolled over to his side, pulling the bear fur higher and settled. His mind wouldn't rest.

Now he was a business owner, a proprietor of a popular trading post on the trail from White Pass summit to Sitka. Tedero imparted as much as he could in the weeks they spent together, and he knew he would depend on Kimalu and his wife when it came to furs and judging gold for payment. Learning many new things, finding his place, exactly what he went in search of when he left Nebraska.

CHAPTER FIVE

A whine outside the cabin door had him rolling over. It sounded like Aitii wanted in, but he knew the sled dogs were never allowed inside. They usually curled up tightly, stuck their nose in their fluffy tail, and slept through the worst of it. But there it was again, this time accompanied by a howl. Maybe she was lonely without the other dogs, although he found that difficult to believe. He'd been told Huskies were independent and could feed themselves year around if on their own. Slipping out and padding across the cooling floor, he removed the wide wooden beam bracing the door closed and peered out to chastise the dog or let her in, depending on how sympathetic she appeared.

"What is it, girl?" Instead of the instantaneous blur of fur he thought he would face charging inside, Aitii jumped away from the door barking into the woods. When he stayed inside the cabin, she came back and repeated her antics. He had heard about how smart these dogs were and that they used a type of howling like a telegraph, so he felt he needed to follow her. Something or someone was outside between him and the river, causing Aitii all sorts of worry.

Hurrying inside, he quickly pulled on all the layers he recently had removed plus grabbing the loaded rifle. No one went outside in Alaska without a weapon to defend themselves.

Aitii was waiting impatiently right outside the door and whined again before running howling into the woods. No answering howls in return so it wasn't a dog team stuck somewhere. He trudged on. The snow wasn't deep, but it was cold. He kept as much of his face covered against the frigid air as he could and still see. Aitii bounded out in front of him, stopping and sniffing a pile on the ground.

"What did you find?" He hurried to the snow-covered bundle to find it was furs. When he lifted it, he found it to be a parka. Now why would someone discard their parka? Aitii was off again barking, coaxing him to follow. In the gloom, he could just make out the dog ahead of him but couldn't move as quickly, even though she was keeping her pace slower so he could keep up.

Then there was a flurry of whining as Aitii pushed her nose into yet another pile in the snow, jumping around it and making little yips and trying to bite what was there. He reached the lump and realized it was a person, a boy by the size of him, and Matthew kept Aitii from biting at the boy anymore while trying to figure out if he was dead or alive. Finally deciding he would take him back to the cabin either way, Matthew managed to lift the boy, now wrapped in the parka, and carry the rifle for the trek back through the trees to the still-dark log building. Aitii was now quieter, but still bouncing excitedly by his side licking the bare hand hanging down near Matthew's waist.

Placing what felt like a frozen bundle on the floor in front of the stove, he felt for signs of life. There was none, and the fetal position made it difficult to test a mirror in front of the boy's nose to see if he was still breathing. The body was so cold it seemed to be permanently curled with his extremities pulled as close to his body as possible.

Matthew knew what to do—or had heard what he should do. He shoved more wood into the stove and began to remove the stiff clothes from his guest. Those were wet and frozen, as if the boy had swum somewhere along his way. Gently he pulled off the boots, but he wasn't wearing the usual underlayers, just the sealskin boots with lacings. He checked the toes for frostbite then moved the boy enough to pull off his shirt and noticed how blue the lips and eyelids were as well as the fingers.

The boy couldn't be very old, his nails, fingers, and arm muscles seemed unused to hard work. He pulled off the next two layers without waking the boy at all, and as he tried to move him to remove the boy's pants, Matthew sat back, lifting his own hands into the air. My God, there were breasts! Female breasts. He didn't have a boy; he had a young woman. Quickly pushing all other thoughts from his mind, he finished undressing her and shoved her under his bed covers. Still no movement, not even a quiver of an eyelash.

Matthew knew what he was supposed to do now. But he never thought about saving a woman, a very attractive young woman, in that manner. She was so still he wondered if she had died while he tried to care for her. Urgency had him stripping down to just the bottom portion of his long johns and sliding in beside her. He knew he was supposed to be naked as well so that he could share his body heat, but that seemed just wrong with her not being able to agree to it.

Wrapping himself around her, his body pulled

away unconsciously. It was like holding a block of ice up against his entire body, although his legs felt a little better than his chest. But that was a problem. It meant she wasn't benefiting from his heat as much as she could, so he lifted his hips and pushed his long johns to the bottom of the covers, freeing his skin to give all the benefit it could to warming the woman. If holding an icicle up to his crotch didn't tamp down any need his body came up with, then nothing would.

His bedmate was soon racked with shudders and shivers as her body grew more accustomed to the warmth. Her legs and arms relaxed against his but were still shaking with the need for heat. Promising himself he wouldn't sleep so that he could jump out of the bed as soon as she recovered, he lay holding her, making sure he wasn't touching any part of her he didn't need to, and fell asleep.

Waking, he found a warm body pressed up against him. He closed his eyes and gently made an inventory of available body parts to assure himself she had become warm and was generating her own heat as well. He was careful not to touch her breasts or any area considered different from his own body which, thankfully, was behaving as a gentleman. Lorelei would have been proud of his restraint and his brothers would have teased him over it.

He was convinced his guest could be left now. He opened his eyes to be met with wide-open lavender eyes edged with black lashes. If anyone had tried to describe the shade to him, he would think they were lying, but they were darn near purple.

"Ah-h-h, don't be frightened. I was just leaving now that you're warm again. Do you mind, um, shutting your eyes while I get out and dressed?"

"You are an American, *nyet*?" She didn't move or shove him away in maidenly modesty. He was particularly glad she hadn't started screaming, since he didn't think he knew what to do with a screaming woman of any age.

"Oh, good, you speak English. I was afraid I would need to explain what happened, and it was going to be much easier in my own language. I don't know enough Russian yet, although my friend Tedero taught me enough to get by with the trappers and miners." He knew he was babbling and hoped his brain kept up with his mouth and he didn't say anything embarrassing—for him.

If she thought it odd to hold a conversation like this while being naked with a stranger, she didn't seem to notice. Wait! Perhaps she was a prostitute. Tedero said women up here were either married or a prostitute, sometimes both. But married women were rarely without their husbands unless left at home with their children. So, which was she—married or prostitute?

"I, ah, I still should get up and see to the stove. Maybe get us something to eat?"

She placed her small warm hand on his wrist. "Thank you for taking me in. I would have frozen to death without your help."

"Ah, it was nothing. I mean, I'm sure anyone else would have done the same thing. I think I did it right, I mean, warmed you up correctly and all…" He knew he was beginning to sweat. Not just because the stove had heated the cabin up warmer than he usually kept it, but because his body parts were beginning to urge him to settle back down and hold a conversation with the woman. Maybe she wanted to thank him. Who knows?

"It was everything, American. You did it perfectly. Many think to leave the clothes on, but it acts as insulation, and the dressed body does not warm up. I had no body heat to keep in at that point, and I am grateful you shared yours with me."

"Sure, I mean, it was no hardship after all…I mean I'd do it anytime…I…I better stop talking. I'm new to Alaska, so I find some of the customs strange."

"You mean the Eskimo practice of sharing their women? Are you married?"

He felt heat suffuse his neck and face. "No." Not sure where she was going with this question. He was trying to get ahead of her and decide what his answer would be. He knew some of the tribes up here offered their women, even wives, to visitors passing through, but wasn't sure what he thought of the idea before. Never thought it would happen to him.

She burst his daydream bubble. "Then you will probably never be offered a woman. You see, it is usually a reciprocal arrangement. You share your woman with the host, and he allows you to borrow his. Even if you were travelling alone, the host would expect to sleep with your wife when he visited you."

"Th-that's very interesting, but I wasn't thinking of that at all." Her vivid eyes never left his gaze, and he knew she was trying not to laugh at his gushing lie. "Not really, not at first. You mentioned it first, I think."

Placing her hand over his lips, she shook her head. "American, I do not need you to explain anything. A woman knows some things instinctively. Go and make breakfast and see if any of my clothes are dry. The last thing I remember was falling through what I thought was a frozen stream. Lucky for me, it was still in the shallows, and I climbed up the bank and continued on."

"Sure thing, ah, about that turning around?"

He heard her cover her head while giggling at his embarrassment, but it was enough to get him dressing as fast as he ever had, leaving his woven, grass moccasins for last. Turning, he found her head still covered, and he called over his shoulder, "You can breathe now." He began checking the clothes he hastily laid out the night before to dry and found them ready to wear once more. "What do you want for breakfast? I make great biscuits and gravy."

"My clothes first. I need to heed the call of nature as you American's say." She grabbed the clothes he tossed to her, and she disappeared beneath the furs to dress. Now why hadn't he thought of that?

Well-fed and holding hot cups of coffee, they remained sitting at the table talking.

"American, you must go by another name, or should I give you one?"

"No, I should have introduced myself when we woke up, but, as you surmised, I was a little off-balanced at finding such a beautiful woman in my bed." He felt he could tease her now that they were both fully dressed and sitting as friends. "I'm Matthew Foster of Whitewater Rapids, Nebraska in the fine United States of America."

She brightened. "Is that near the city of Bellevue? I've been there by train, but it was on a trip to a place called Chicago. It was beautiful there with this huge lake and no whales."

"Nebraska? Oh, yes, you mean Chicago and the Great Lake. No, more toward the western half and before leaving for Alaska, I was never more than twenty miles from home."

"It is good to meet you, Matthew Foster. I'm Katarina Petrovna, of St. Petersburg, Russia."

He hesitated but really needed to know about how she got here in the middle of the night. "Do you want to tell me about yesterday? How you ended up half-dressed outside the trading post?"

"I suppose that would make you curious. I feel very foolish because part of it was my fault. My fault for not seeing the danger right in front of me." She gnawed her bottom lip, which was still blistered from the cold, and he rose, giving her time to find the words. He feared she was in trouble but didn't allow his mind to run wild because there were all sorts of ways a young beautiful woman could get into trouble in Alaska. Bringing back a jar of salve, he pointed to her lips, and she nodded, acknowledging what it was for.

"I was staying with my great aunt waiting for my father to return from a trip with the mushers and teams further north. There is this man, Ivan Gallavanoff, who thinks he should be my husband. I have told him over and over again I do not wish to marry him, but he says his mother, who had the sight, declared it to him right down to the color of my eyes. I have never met the woman, but Ivan is sure she meant me. I am to be his bride, and together, we will rule a large nation. He thinks she meant Russia."

"Can't he go back to his mother and get more information? If you don't want to marry the man, then it must be someone else he makes his life with."

"His mother died years ago. He is living on memories of what she said. I think it is too long of winter, too much time alone, and too much vodka that has his thinking all mixed up."

"So, you were trying to stay away from him? Got lost?"

"*Da* and *nyet* to both. As I say, we were left in a cabin and had just taken a bath. My Aunt Alexandria was beginning to dry my hair when this big brute of a man breaks down the door and begins to rant and rave about how I must marry him. That it is time, and we must be married so he can become czar. I told him he was crazy and to leave my father's house.

"Instead of leaving, he becomes mean and violent, saying he will take me, and we will marry when we reach Russia, that his mother, who you remember is dead, told him to get me with child. He tried reaching for me, and I kept out of his way, trying to talk sense into him, but he would not listen. It was like he was mad. He even began to drool and almost had me when my aunt yelled for me to run out the door. She had a palm-sized Deringer pointed on him, but it had only one shot.

"Ivan stopped making the deep growling sounds and seemed focused on the weapon, although I wasn't sure how much real damage it could do through his layers of furs. I stomped my feet into my boots and grabbed my parka before he thought things through or tried to yank the gun from her. I did not like to leave Aunt Alexandria, but what else could I do? He didn't want her, hardly paid her any attention. That is why she could get to her muff pistol without him noticing."

"And you just kept running?"

"I didn't want to go back in case he stayed, and I didn't want to take the trail toward my father for fear

Ivan would catch me up on the trail with his team. I went in a direction different from one we usually take, although I knew there was a trading post in this direction. I thought I could make it, but not with wet hair and without the proper gear. I am so grateful you found me before I lost any toes or fingers."

"Aitii, the husky with me, let me know you were out there. I just followed her and brought you back."

"Still, it was more than many would do for a stranger. You endangered your own life going out in the freezing night looking for who knows what."

He poured them both more coffee. The large purple bruises on her upper arms gave credence to her story if he even needed any. "I'm glad I did. Do you live here now, in Alaska?"

"I'm travelling with my father. He's trading for furs. As a member of the royal family, we are welcome everywhere. My family is involved in many businesses."

"He's a trapper?" It seemed strange, but he knew the Russians were once the majority of people in Alaska besides the native tribes, and Russian royalty were widespread.

"No, more than that. More of a distributor, a middleman, so to speak. He owns a fleet of ships that sail between here and Russia. He brings vodka, brandy and whiskey, knives, cookware, rifles and bullets, anything he can make a profit on. He's here to trade with the Alaskan natives for furs. The seal pelt is becoming popular, but still, fox, ermine, mink, and sable are the most sought. My papa accepts only the best. Polar bear, seal, sea otter—all to take back to Russia."

His mind had stopped at one fact. Her father must be rich as well as having royal blood. Could the gulf between them get any wider? "A fleet of ships? Like how many?"

"A couple of dozen. They come and go all over the world and bring back all sorts of things from the east to the west and the west to the east. He has whole warehouses in several ports filled with things people want. And he has stables of horses and wagons to move the inventory anywhere in Russia. He is a very busy man."

"And I suppose a prince as well?"

"But, of course,"—she giggled—"or I wouldn't be a princess."

She spoke of being royalty in such easy terms, as if everyone was a prince or princess. Probably where she came from, they were, but to him, she was so far above him he felt humbled that she would even stop long enough to speak with him.

Embarrassed to even be thinking such things, he stood again. "Why don't we kit you out with what you'll need to get back home. We wouldn't want your aunt to think you got eaten by a bear."

"She always says I would get spit out because I am so tough. Papa says it would be because I am such a little bite and not worth chewing." She laughed when she told him that, and he realized her family was like any other. They teased and cared for one another, and they would worry. He couldn't figure out how to get a message to them so they wouldn't. Another problematic part of living in Alaska—no telegraph.

"You cook quite well. You haven't always been on your own." Katarina wiped the bottom of her bowl with

41

the crust of the sourdough bread and popped it neatly into her mouth.

"No, my ma wasn't well near the end, and I had six brothers who needed feeding. The youngest not much more than a baby. My oldest brother, Luke, was doing everything he could to keep the ranch running. We all did our part, but as next to the oldest, the cooking fell on me. Nothing fancy, although I can fry southern-style chicken and make a great pot of ham and beans."

Smiling and nodding, she finished her meal. "They both sound good, but chicken will be difficult to find in Alaska. They find it too cold, I think."

"Probably, we kept them for eggs mostly, but in the fall, you need to kill off the older ones. Even in Nebraska, they stop laying as many eggs when it gets cold."

"Tell me more of these brothers? You sound like you love them, possibly miss them."

A statement, not a question. This woman would know too much about him if he didn't watch what he said around her.

"Yes, we were a close bunch, but it was time for me to move on. Luke got married and was going to have a baby, the others were looking to the future, weddings, going to college. I felt I should move on if I was ever going to do so. Alaska sounded like the right place for me right now. In the future? Who knows?"

"Luke's wife…what about her? Was she nice?"

He knew this woman was too perceptive. Talk about having the "sight." How did she figure out there was something there with Lorelei and Luke and him? "Um, Lorelei? She was wonderful. The younger boys took to her right away. Of course, they didn't remember ma much, and Luke's wife was very caring, very wise. She was good for all of us." He moved to take her bowl to the washbasin, but she stopped him.

"I'll wash the dishes. You made the meal, and it was very good."

"The trap lines always have something in them, and as Suu told me, everything is edible. Fry it up, add some water and flour to the drippings to make gravy, and boil rice. I find it works with almost everything. Been tempted to feed some to Aitii, but Kimalu says to only feed her fish." He was talking to keep her mind off asking anything more about Lorelei. He thought he was over her, but there was something that hurt deep in his heart when her name came up in his mind or conversation.

As he added more wood to the fire, Katarina pulled out the bedding and unrolled it in the open space in front of the stove. She removed some of her outer clothes but left the insulated underwear on before climbing between the furs. Matthew felt relieved to have that question answered before it got embarrassing. They were to share a bed, but not their bodies. He could do this. He would have to remind himself she was a princess and too far out of reach for him, even if he were a man of business and landowner. Somehow, it didn't seem like much of an accomplishment anymore.

CHAPTER SIX

Matthew laid in the fur bed, one arm behind his head, trying to ignore the soft body lying so still next to him. Katarina had fallen asleep almost immediately again. It had been the same for the past four nights without any change. He stayed wide awake, fearing he would end up cuddling or spooning her. Either way, his body wouldn't keep his secret, and his reaction to having her in bed with him would frighten her, he was sure. She was used to Alaskan ways, but he was pretty sure any man she had slept beside was a family member. He knew sharing a bed was common, but that didn't include any sexual activity.

She muttered, and then he felt her hand on his bare chest where she moved her fingers tentatively. "Matthew?"

He didn't speak in case his voice squeaked like a teenager going through puberty. "Hm-m-m?"

"You are awake again. Why can't you sleep at night? You are beginning to look, um, haggard."

He couldn't help but answer sarcastically. "Thank you for noticing, but I sleep. I sleep every night."

"But not well. Let me help you sleep."

His entire body tensed. She was an innocent. He would bet his last dollar on it, and she didn't know what she was saying. She couldn't know how a man might interpret her offer. "I told you, I'll sleep eventually." He went to roll over giving her his back to rub against if she felt cold.

"No, turn toward me. It's better this way—warmer."

"Tonight, I think this is better." He tried to roll away again, but she dug her fingers into the hair of his chest and held on. "Katarina, what are you doing? I know you're innocent, but you're not stupid."

"No, I am not, but one of us is. I have waited for you to decide when we make love, but my father will find me soon now, and we still haven't been together as a man and woman."

"And I don't plan on us doing so. Katarina, you are a desirable, beautiful woman who will one day marry and have a family. I don't want you to regret throwing away something precious on the likes of me."

"I like the 'likes' of you, Matthew. I know what is right for me, when is right for me—it is you, and it is now. I ran from Ivan because he was not the one, I ran from others because they were not the ones. You, Matthew Foster, you are the one, I choose."

"No, don't say such things, please." He couldn't help liking what she said. That she desired him as he did her, but that didn't make it right. He needed to keep things proper between them.

"You like me, I know you do, just as I like you—more than like, but we won't need to say the words because they will get in the way. Tonight, is for us to enjoy one another. I will never regret this night, I promise."

She leaned across him and covered his mouth with hers sucking gently. Without thinking, his arms came around her body and held her to him as he devoured her with his mouth, breaking from her lips only to kiss and suck her neck and behind her ear. She turned the tables and laved his ear, causing a euphoric sensation tingling down his spine.

Rolling on top of her, he molded one breast with his hand while kissing her mouth, slipping his tongue into her and dueling with hers. Her hands roamed his chest, playing in his chest hair before mapping every inch of him. He reached to her waist and pulled off the long-sleeved top baring her to him. His mouth covered one breast while the other gently massaged the other nipple to a peak. Then he switched to enjoy licking the other breast. Katarina arched into him, moaning for more.

How could he ignore her pleas? How could any man ignore a woman needing what he could give her? He slid his hand into her union suit and found the curl-covered mound. If he stopped now, he could assure her safety. If he continued to pleasure her, he could lose control and not regain sanity enough to stop before it went too far. He couldn't find the strength to deny what she was pleading him for—couldn't stop himself.

Sliding a finger into her, he felt her thighs clench around his hand. Kissing her again, she relaxed and allowed him to move within her warm, silky channel. The feel of her almost unmanned him, but he decided on a plan and braced himself to follow it through. He would give her what she asked for—he would give her relief.

Rocking against her outer thigh, Matthew entered and withdrew his finger, finding the growing bud begging for his touch. Katarina's breathing was as fast and as heavy as his, and he knew what she was feeling.

That deep need tightening every muscle in her body, the spiraling like a spring winding ever tighter until she couldn't take it another minute…And there it was! She was gasping and holding him and panting for breath and shuddering to a quivering end.

He kissed her and moved her to his side as she caught her breath. "Matthew, what did you do? That was, that was so, so…"

Grinning like a fool, he felt quite proud he could bring her to an orgasm and righteously feel he did her no harm. Nothing for her to look back on and regret. "Sh-h-h-h, go to sleep now, and quit bothering me. We have a lot of work to do in the morning."

"But…"

"No buts, just sleep." He was still staring at the rafters when her soft little breaths told him she had finally listened to something he told her and went to sleep.

The next day, neither of them said anything about the night before. Matthew had promised to be stronger in his resistance to her requests while still trying to spend time with her while she was there. Her reminding him that her father would be coming any day to sweep her away didn't have him sleeping any better than he had been. In fact, it probably worked in the other direction. Now, he not only worried about trying to keep his hands off her, he worried that he wouldn't have enough time to show her how much he cared about her. How much he wanted to be more to her. More than just the man who happened to find her freezing in the snow.

After making a meal and setting a pan of beans to soak, he made sure Katarina had everything from his supplies and stock to keep her warm enough, including a pair of snowshoes. Needing to check the trap lines, for some reason, he felt better taking her with him rather than leaving her alone in the post where anyone could find her. Aitii would follow Matthew so that she could investigate what had been moving through her area which would leave Katarina on her own.

"Are you ready? Do you need to practice with these?" he asked, as he finished tying the bulky shoe onto her mukluks.

"No, I've worn these for years. It feels funny the first time every year, but then it becomes second nature, and I can make very good time."

Smiling, he opened the door then locked it behind him as usual. "That's good, because the trap line isn't very long, but it may take a while if there are many animals to harvest. Then I'll be busy in the tanning shed getting the fur processed and the meat ready for eating."

"I don't like muskrat, so don't bother making that for me. Marmot is good, though, I think they are hibernating right now. Rabbit is tasty, and I have a good recipe for that..."

He wondered if she would continue to talk the whole way and then realized he didn't care. In fact, he hoped she would keep talking since soon he wouldn't have her voice in his ear at all. Soon her father would arrive and take her back with him. Take her someplace he would never see her again or hear her light chatter with its endearing accent and unusual rhythm.

There wasn't a muskrat, but there were a couple of rabbits, so Matthew thought he would gain some esteem in her eyes. It wasn't anything much to brag about, but at least he showed her he could provide for her. Could keep her fed, at least, even if it was animals caught in a trap rather than raised like the cattle back in Nebraska. Between the cattle and trading with neighbors, most of the family's needs were covered as far as food went. Cash was needed for clothing and shoes, but everything else had been up to his brother to furnish.

Lorelei had been sewing much of the boys clothing when he left, and probably still was, so even that expense had been cut back. If someone could make boots out of the cowhides from their own cattle, they wouldn't need money for anything except paying the bank back on the mortgage.

Katarina called out as she marched to the trading post. "It looks like someone's been here, Matthew. See these tracks?"

"Yeah, you're right, but they didn't try to hide them. Maybe someone was going to stay, but when we weren't here decided to keep going to the water. They could have made Copper Harbor at the edge of the intercoastal if they were a good walker."

Nodding, she took the key from him and unlocked the door. Aitii began barking and ran toward the tanning shed where Matthew was destined for next. An old man came out appearing frightened by Aitii's actions and then smiled when he saw Matthew and Katarina. He was thin, even wearing the bulky furs needed for warmth this time of year. His face was covered by a white beard and bushy brows, nearly hid his eyes. He became animated as he realized there were others there besides the dog.

"Oh, good, someone is here. I came to see my friend Tedero and swap stories with him. I try to do that once a year while he's here during the winter months. He spends his time in town during the warm months, and that's my busiest time." Seeming to see both Matthew and Katarina were surprised by his appearance, he stopped and asked, "Did I miss him already? Isn't it still winter?" He peered around him as if the snow would melt away and green leaves would spring from the still hibernating branches.

Katarina was the first to recover and realize the man was no danger. "Yes, it is still winter, and you didn't miss Tedero as much as Tedero didn't stay here this winter. Instead, he returned to Russia and sold the post to this man. His name is Matthew Foster."

Matthew stepped forward, putting out his hand to shake the man's, and spoke. "I'm glad you came for a visit. I hold to the same rules of hospitality that my good friend did. Are you hungry? Would you like to come in and get warm? I left the stove burning, so it wouldn't take much to get the coffee going."

The man seemed confused at so much coming at him. "I, ah, I don't think I'm hungry. I trap a lot during the winter like what you've got there." He nodded to the rabbits and minks. "I get plenty of meat, but no one to talk with. Unless I begin talking to the animals…the live ones, not the dead ones, I bring in from the traps." He laughed at his own joke, and Matthew glanced over to see an expression of sorrow pass over Katarina's face.

She spoke quietly, "I will see to getting that coffee, sir. Would you like to go with Matthew to the tanning shed? It's the building that you just came out of."

"Oh, yes, yes, it is. Tedero and I spent quite a bit of time working on furs and pelts together. At one time, there were so many mink around here it was easy to end up with enough for a full-length coat each winter. Of course, there were other furs just as rich and thick. We couldn't get enough sable to send back to Russia, although we made a dent in the sable population. Now there's real hunting involved in getting sable."

The two men went into the shed, still warmed from the sun which had been shining all day. One reason Matthew had taken Katarina with him. The possibility a stranger would come by had been another. Thankfully, this man didn't seem dangerous, although he seemed to have difficulty with reality. Not simply that Tedero wasn't there where the man evidently expected him to be, but it was the way he said things. As if the past and the future and the present were swirling around him. That he had difficulty with what exactly was happening, and even when. Matthew would have bet the man didn't know what year it was. He may not even be aware that the United States now owned Alaska. He would use subtle questions to find out how safe the man was to be out on his own.

After skinning the animals and doing the first process of getting the fur taken care of, both men came into the cabin to the smell of something delicious cooking.

"I thought it best to start supper, Matthew, so you wouldn't have to wait for your meal." She asked, seeming to try to get more information about their guest, "Is, ah, is your friend staying?"

"Yes, Katarina, this is, Abe. Abe has been in these mountains since he was sixteen, but he's not sure how long ago that was. He met Tedero years later when Tedero built this post on the site of an older one set up by another Russian." That was as much information as he felt he could give her at one time. Abe, although a loner most of the time, must save up all his talking for this one visit to Tedero, and since that man wasn't here, then all the talk saved was now for Matthew.

"Do you want these rabbits in here, or should I keep them cold outside?"

"No, I've already made up the flour coating. I fry them in oil once I've dusted them with the flour mixture. It's best with egg, too, although we don't have any eggs left. We will need to wait till spring, I think."

Matthew backed Katarina's facts. "Yeah, I guess we can get frozen ones from town, but only if they have some left. Otherwise, we need to wait for the chickens to come from Russia this spring."

"I used to have chickens. Or my ma did at one point. She made the best fried chicken..." Abe added to the conversation, and Katarina smiled at him.

She spoke slowly but not unkindly, as if to a child. "I think the best food is always served at our mother's table. I know my favorites were hers, as well."

"My ma must be dead by now, wouldn't you think? I don't know for sure..." Since the man was seventy, if he was a day, Matthew thought the man's mother would have passed, but who was he to bring that truth home? If the man wanted to think there was a chance his mother was at home cooking fried chicken, then it didn't hurt anyone for him to do so.

Another message was passed between Matthew and Katarina as she took the rabbit from him and began cutting it up on the large cutting table into pieces for cooking. The sizzle soon told him the meat had been added to the oil, and the fragrance of garlic and pepper filled the air along with the browning meat.

Even Abe sniffed the air appreciatively. "Yep, fried chicken. I can taste it already."

As they ate, neither reminded the man he was eating rabbit and not chicken, but they all enjoyed it along with the flavorful beans. Matthew tried to figure out what she had done to them, but they tasted better than anything he had ever done to them. He made a mental note to ask later in case she added something Abe would remember his mother did, too.

Nighttime was well upon them, and everyone looked toward their beds as the kitchen was cleaned up and the bones tossed out the door for Aitii to bury.

"Since you're staying Abe, why don't you sleep next to the stove over here. You should be comfortable," Matthew offered, wanting to keep the man farthest from Katarina.

"Thank you, son, I think I will. It's mighty nice of you both to take pity on an old-timer like myself. Tedero taught you well." The man laid down and pulled a fur over his clothes. All but his hat, which he had removed hours ago and hung on a peg by the door along with his long rifle.

Matthew had relaxed quite a bit once the man had set his weapon aside. He was trying to figure out how he was going to protect Katarina while giving the man the hospitality he knew Tedero would expect him to.

Whispering to one another, knowing the old man's hearing was poor, he told her, "I think he's lonely. He doesn't talk about his life as it is now, but he's used to being in that shed. Knew where everything was kept."

"I have seen older people like this. I hope that he finds a way to go into a town where people can look out for him. Sitka might be too rough, but there are smaller places. You know, where a man might not get lost so easily. Where people won't take advantage of him."

"I know, but he seems happy to be still on his own. Happy to be a trapper in a world where the trappers are traveling hundreds of miles a year to keep pace with where the fur animals are. Earlier, the seals were north of Sitka, and now no one knows where they are for sure. The man who works here sometimes is out whale hunting, I think. Dangerous work, but one whale will feed a whole village for a year."

"Yes, I know. I have grown up knowing these people and how much their lives have changed."

Chuckling, he nodded, "Sometimes I forget how long you've been here while I'm the newcomer. The *cheechako* to be made fun of."

"No, after your time here this winter, no one can call you a *cheechako*. Not and have anything to support the disparaging remark."

"If Abe leaves tomorrow as he intends, I'll make sure he has everything he needs."

"And I'll make sure he is well-fed." He slid closer to her, allowing this touching since the old man's presence would prevent Matthew from doing anything more. A little petting and cooing would be allowed, but he wanted to leave her as innocent as when she arrived.

After breakfast, the old man was still there, and Katarina told him, "If you're staying for a while, I will make you *akutaq*. It's Eskimo ice cream." Matthew's brows rose remembering the sweet creamy dessert of his youth. Every Fourth of July someone would get out an ice cream maker, and the men would take turns cranking it. With six brothers, it took a while to make enough for all of them with the younger ones getting their portion first and the others eating in shifts as the salt and ice froze the fresh cream with sweet berries. His mouth watered, and he couldn't believe he hadn't thought of making some sooner than this.

Taking a large bowl, Katarina scooped new snow then drizzled seal oil onto it. Taking her clean hand, she began whipping it around and around. At first, he saw no difference, but then he realized, just like the ice cream crank, the snow began to solidify the oil as she went faster and faster with her hand stirring the mixture against the cold sides of the bowl and mixing in the snow.

Licking his lips, he could almost taste the confection and remembered his favorite strawberry ice cream with fresh sweet berries just picked from the garden. As he opened his eyes, he saw her add some little pink berries. Not the rich, dark red ones of his youth, but beggars can't be choosers, after all. Whatever they were, they were now part of the mixture and sure to be as addictive as he had always found ice cream.

She served a small bowl out to Abe who took one mouthful and let his eye roll to the top of his head. "That's perfect, my dear. Absolutely perfect."

Matthew couldn't wait and stuck his finger into the bowl taking a large dollop onto it before plunging it into his mouth. His eyes widened, and he covered his mouth so that the rancid tasting stuff wasn't spewed all over Katarina and their guest. How could the man think this was good? How could he have forgotten what ice cream tasted like?

"What is wrong, Matthew? Why are your eyes

tearing up?" She followed him outside where he spit and spit and spit. Finally wiping his hand over his tongue, he glared at her in accusation.

"What is that?" His dream of tasting the sweet pink-tinged favorite of his past died. "It tastes like lard with fish in it."

"Oh, Matthew, I thought you knew about the *akutaq*. I didn't know this was the first time you tasted it. It isn't like American ice cream, not at all."

"I realize that now. What is in that? It tastes like fish and not in a good way."

Laughing, she didn't appear to be sorry at all. "I am sorry, Matthew. The snow makes the oil solidify, and then salmonberries, which actually taste like fish, are added, or sometimes seeds and bits of fish even. I had no idea you didn't know what it was. It was a treat for Abe. He said he was partial to it last night."

"I guess I missed that part of the conversation," he said, shaking his head before pulling her to him. "I deserve a kiss after that."

"No, I don't think so," she teased, "You taste of fish." Then giggled and ran back into the cabin while he looked down at his mukluks laughing. Well, that showed him who the *cheechako* was.

CHAPTER SEVEN

Their guest had left saying he was going on to Copper Harbor where he was sure to find a bed for a few nights with friends. The two waved the man off earlier in the day, telling him he could come back and visit anytime. Matthew wasn't sure the old man realized that Katarina wasn't his wife or that the next time Abe returned she wouldn't be there. Only her memory.

Katarina had been quiet for the past hour giving him surreptitious glances when she thought he wasn't watching. She was making plans for this night, and he was trying to keep from taking her completely as his body was telling him to do. It was one thing to forego release himself one night, but night after night of sleeping next to her after pleasuring her was going to push his limits.

His mind was on that night, on her body, and their needs when the door burst open slamming against the wall before stopping. Looking up, Matthew saw a mammoth of a man covered in furs from top to toe bellowing, "Where is she? What have you done with her? I will kill you if you have touched her!"

Instinctively, Matthew stepped forward putting himself between Katarina and the menacing danger filling the doorway. He glanced at the loaded rifle hanging above the man's head on the wall and wished he'd planned ahead better.

Bravely, Katarina shouted, "Ivan, go away. I told you we are never going to be wed. You and I are not destined to be together. I have my own visions, and I am with this man." She pointed at Matthew who still faced the unprovoked intruder.

The man's mouth opened as a roar erupted shaking the bottles on the shelves before lumbering toward Matthew, throwing them both to the wooden floor. Matthew twisted and quickly stood realizing that although he could move easier without the heavy burden of parkas and boots, the other man was harder to wrestle down. Not only did he outweigh Matthew by more than double, the furs the other man wore made it impossible to get a good hold on his attacker.

Matthew was strong and wiry from years of carrying feed sacks, fence posts, and calves to branding. He knew his strength and skill at wrestling with his brothers, but that was in play and not life and death. Matthew knew the man getting up off the floor wasn't going to hold back anything. He was going to go for Matthew's throat.

Grunting, the man lowered his head and rammed into Matthew's middle carrying him along and into the log wall. The air left Matthew's lungs while he tried to keep his feet under him. Another thrust against the wall and Matthew felt his wrist snap, and pain streaked through his arm and upper body as if hit by lightning. Sliding to the floor, his vision became blurry when he felt a pain go through the back of his head at the same time. He thought he saw Katarina moving closer.

Wanting to warn her away, he tried to move his head and found it unresponsive. He was at the mercy of the huge man standing over him and that man's huge fist ready to pummel him. Then there was an odd metallic thud, and the giant tumbled in a pile half covering Matthew's splayed legs.

Trying to make sense of things and tell Katarina to run, he became aware the behemoth was moving and coming to his senses. Matthew tried to rally himself, digging deeply for what strength he could find to fight the man giving Katarina enough time to escape.

"Ivan Gallavanoff, get away from him. I am his wife in every sense of the word, and you coming in here saying otherwise will not make it so. Get out, or my father will hunt you down and gut you like a salmon. Get it out of your head that we will ever wed." She held the large metal frying pan in the air menacingly.

"Nyet, Katarina, do not say such things. We are meant to be together, and this man, this man will fade in your memory."

"No, I would never forget the man I gave my virtue to, the man I love beyond reason. You must get this through your thick skull, or I will strike you again until you do concede."

"But we are destined…"

"Never. I have told you over and over, we are not to be together. Not in this life and not in the next."

The large man rolled to his knees, and then, with the help of the sturdy meat table, grappled to his feet. "You have given yourself to this puny man?"

"I have and I have no regrets." She stood proudly and did not back down even when the man seemed about to make a grab for her. "Leave before I hit you again, before my father finds you."

"My mother must have read the signs wrong. No woman who was supposed to marry me would hit me with a frying pan, no woman who was supposed to marry me would give herself willingly to another. I spit on your memory." Then he spat and lumbered out through the door, which Katarina threw closed and lifted the heavy wooden post into place.

Dropping down beside him on the floor, she gently felt his head finding the sore spot. "I think you will be all right, but you will have a headache for days. I'm so sorry he hurt you."

He half-smiled. "I'm glad you were here to protect me. I was foolish enough to try to get to the rifle when I had a whole wall of fry pans behind me. Maybe you should make the decisions on how to fight our battles."

"Does your nose hurt? It looks as if it took a hit, too."

"It feels like all of me took a hit, but I think I may have a broken arm or, hopefully, only my wrist." He held up his right hand which was already turning purple and swelling.

"Oh, no, let me get some snow. It will help with the pain…"

"Take the rifle with you, and be careful." He winced as he tried to stand. He didn't know which hurt worse, his arm or his head. While she was outside, he made it to the table and sat in one of the two chairs.

He was relieved to see her enter with a bowl of snow and lean the rifle against the wall before coming to him. "If we lay your wrist down and then a cloth and put the snow around it…hopefully, it will help."

He allowed her to check the back of his head and pronounce it swollen and bruised, also. They were trying to figure a way to put snow on it when once again the door burst open, banging back against the wall. A behemoth of a man attired in grey and brown furs from top to toe bellowed, "Where is she? What have you done with her? I will kill you if you have touched her!"

Matthew didn't know where he would find the strength, but he wouldn't allow anyone to take Katarina against her will. He tucked his injured arm inside his shirt against his chest for protection. The last man almost knocked him out with a single lunge. He eyed the rifle leaning next to the door and tried to make a plan to reach it before he was beaten to a pulp. He sent a silent prayer as he planted his feet getting ready for the assault, ready to take the man's full weight as he attacked.

A colorful blur swept past him and into the giant's arms as the intruder picked Katarina off the floor and dangled her midair as if he held a snowflake.

"Papa, Papa, I was so frightened. Ivan came after me and wouldn't take no for an answer. I warned him you would find me if he didn't let me go." Hiccupping sobs could be heard muffled into the mountain of fur.

"*Nyet, nyet malysh*, I am here now, and no one will harm you, I promise." With one fierce eye staring at Matthew from the collar of his coat, he added, "And if anyone already has, then I will kill him without regard."

She glanced up and shook her head. "*Nyet*, Papa, Matthew has only been kind to me. He saved my life when I had to run to protect my virtue from Ivan. Ivan needs killing, Papa." Her feet finally touched the floorboards, and she turned, pulling the mammoth behind her to the bench at the table. "This is my papa, Boris Petrovna. Papa, this is Matthew Foster who owns this post now. Tedero is ill and has returned home."

"*Da*, I heard. There are less and less of us old-timers here any longer, *malysh*. I knew this was our last trip when we left Vladivostok, but I didn't wish to tell you. It is why your Aunt Alexandria accompanied us this time. To say goodbye to New Archangel, where she met the man she loved. Your uncle was a good man, a great man to many, but could not face the loss of his adopted home. When we sold Alaska, we sold our souls."

She turned to look at Matthew who sat at the table, once again with his arm covered in the cold, wet cloths. He didn't want her to do anything heroic, telling her father even half the things she said to Ivan to get him to leave. This wasn't a place for a woman like her, not for a princess.

The man stood, saying gruffly, "I must get my sled and team. I left them where I saw signs another had done the same. I thought it might be Ivan but could not be sure. He probably did it for the same reason I did so as not to warn whoever was in the trading post." His sad eyes watched Katarina move to Matthew's side and put more snow on his wrist. "Pack up what you have, *malyutka*, we will leave soon."

Matthew felt a tear drop onto his shoulder and soak into his shirts. He had to say something, tell her how much she meant to him even if they would never see one another again. "What did he call you?"

She answered quietly. "A pet name, it means baby, little one. I told you I get no respect as a woman. They treat me as a child. But I am no longer a child, and he must see that."

"I don't think it a good idea to state it in that manner. I don't think fathers want to think of their, ah, little girls becoming women. I know I would feel the same way."

"But I love you, you know I do, even if we haven't known one another very long. Love isn't based on time. My Aunt Alexandria met her husband in a snowstorm, and they made love that night. When my father found her, he nearly killed my uncle before Alexandria could protect him and offer to marry him immediately..."

"I would do the same, except I don't think it will work on your father again. I mean, it sounds as if your aunt and uncle had other things in common. We are as different as chalk and cheese."

"You Americans have such odd ways of saying things. Now Russians, we have proverbs and stories for every occasion. Great drinking songs as well." She smiled, trying to lighten her own mood. He hoped she could because he hated to think of her crying all the way back to Sitka.

The barking of dogs and Aitii's welcome filled the air with noise as he patted her hand. "You should get your outdoor clothes on so you can leave."

She shook her head while getting out a pan and filling it with water from beneath the stove from snow Matthew had gathered the day before. "I will not leave you so soon after being hurt. Your head is not right yet, and you certainly aren't thinking straight."

He knew she was referring to his failure to fight for her against her father, but he had already made the arguments as to why they should not even think of staying together. Nothing that had occurred that day changed his thinking. She needed to return to her life in Russia.

Her father came in huffing, removing his seal fur

gloves. "Do I smell coffee, *malyutka*? I have been crisscrossing this country for days now without making camp. I was at my most northern point when the messenger sent by my sister caught up to me. Then I returned to her to find no one had seen you since you ran out. I was besieged by worry."

"Matthew saved my life, Papa, so we owe him. I would have died if he hadn't found me. I had already gotten to the point of removing my coat and had no mittens or insulation in my boots. I literally ran for my life when Ivan broke in and Aunt Alexandria held him there with her little pistol."

"*Da*, she told me, but I could not believe that man would have the *mykectbo*, the guts to try to force you from my home. He must be mad. Too long in this cold and barren land."

Smiling, she poured him some coffee. "That is much what I said. I told him you would kill him for even trying."

"I would kill anyone who would attempt to harm you, *malyutka*." His gaze met Matthew's over the rim as he drank, his gray beard almost swallowing the cup.

"Papa, I am warning you now. I will not leave Matthew until he is well enough to care for himself. I cannot leave him with only one good arm. It was broken protecting me. You would still be trying to find me if it weren't for Matthew's quick thinking."

Sotto voiced, Matthew added, "And a well-placed frying pan." Which brought a stern look from his beloved. Boris stood in front of his daughter. "I am expecting you to obey me in this, *malyutka*. I can see this man has mesmerized you with his exotic ways, but you are my daughter and must return to St. Petersburg to live your life."

"But Papa, how can I leave him? We will never find one another again."

The Russian prince turned to Matthew for support knowing he would receive it. "She is a princess, and you are what?" He peered around the darkened cabin with the mess of the first fight plainly visible. "An innkeeper at best? Katarina was born to wear jewels and fine furs and silks. You think she should trade that in to serve food to destitute miners? Sweep floors and act like the lowest serf?"

Matthew didn't think that—he knew she was too good for him and certainly too good to be buried in this Podunk trading post on the way to nowhere. "I have already told her to leave. To return to the life she was meant to live."

"Papa, I get a say in my life—in my future. Look what happened because I am not married. You cannot watch over me all the time. I must have freedom at some point."

"But, little one, this is not the time. Once we return to St. Petersburg, you will have your choice of fiancés, of husbands. I will make sure you meet many, many rich noblemen."

"But I love this noble man, Papa. There is not room in my heart for another." Her gaze was on Matthew and his heart bloomed with the emotions she caused to form within him.

"Your father is right, Katarina. I can never give you what you deserve. I'm a son of a pioneer farmer, and I have a wanderlust in me, also. I may seek out adventure, but I wouldn't subject my wife, my family, to living such a vagabond life. Go with your father. He sounds as if he has your best interest at heart."

She moved to him, so close their breath mingled as she gazed up at him making the room a private place for just the two of them. "Do you not love me, Matthew? Do you not care that I will be taken thousands of miles away once he gets me from this cabin?"

"I want what is best for you and that is not to stay here with me. Everything I have is invested in this place, and although it isn't much, it's all I own. I'm not choosing it over you. There would be no choice to make, but it isn't a simple choice between the two. I can never be the man you need, the husband you deserve, the father to your children." He placed his forehead against hers and closed his eyes so he wouldn't see the sadness in hers. "Go with your papa, and be happy—for me. Live the life of a princess and forget this time in your life ever happened."

She whispered, "Will you?"

He wanted to lie, wanted to set her free, but knew he couldn't. "No, I will remember this week, remember you always."

"As I will, Matthew." She continued gazing into his eyes.

God, he loved the way his name sounded on her lips. He wanted to pull her close, hold her tight, keep the time of her leaving at bay. Instead, he stood straighter, breaking the physical touch between their bodies, and the cool air swirled around them once more.

"There, you see *Malysh*, all will be good now. We will need supplies, which I will pay for, of course." He tossed down a large leather bag which landed with a thud on the table. "I would offer you funds for saving my little one, but I know you are a man who would throw it back in my face."

"Perhaps not throw it, but it would not be accepted, either. I would do it all over again even knowing I was going to get the sh…um, tar kicked out of me."

The two men glared at one another, and Matthew decided there and then he would not be the first to look away. Thankfully, Boris did, as he asked his daughter to get dressed warmly and be ready to leave as soon as the provisions were added to his dog sled.

"Papa, you must go to the trading post near the northern river, yet, right?" Her father nodded, watching her with narrowed eyes. "I will stay and help Matthew for a few more days. On your way back, you can pick me up. Matthew's arm will be better by then, and I will not feel so bad about leaving him." She gazed up through her thick lashes and had the temerity to bat them. Matthew could see Boris almost melting under her plea. Matthew would have laughed except permission for her to stay was so important to him and not because he needed help splitting wood. It would allow them a few more days together, a few more days to become used to her leaving him.

"All right, I think. You will not miss the long trek through the rough trails, I think, so stay here in this nice warm cabin. But remember, *malysh*, you stay only as long as it takes me to finish my business and no longer. My ship sails on time as always, and we will be on it. My experience in Russia-America is over. I will, as they say, retire and take time to spend some of my money."

Bouncing like a young child, Katarina squealed, "Thank you, thank you, Papa. You are the best Papa in the world."

Matthew feared she would overdo it and her father would become suspicious about her exuberance to stay on in a ramshackle cabin on the bank of a freezing tributary, but the man never seemed to question his daughter's gratefulness. Matthew wondered how good an actress Katarina really was. Had she used the same technique on him? On Ivan? Did she always act as if she were easily manipulated, placating the men around her to eventually get what she wanted in the first place?

That evening, Matthew finished his meal after everyone else since he was trying to eat neatly with his left hand. "Katarina, you always had me make all the meals. I thought you couldn't cook, but this was very good."

"Da, she can cook good but has no need except when we travel into the wilds like this. Usually, we have a retinue of servants and a French chef all travelling in a caravan of coaches. She likes to cook when we are here staying rough and in Africa when we went on safari even though the local guides were hired to do all the work."

"I was afraid they would add things like termites and other insects. I wanted to know what I was eating." She took his empty bowl and spoon from him. "I let them collect the water from the crocodile-infested water though."

Both he and Boris laughed. "*Malyutka*, you would get lost like a piece of flotsam between their teeth."

"I may not be big like you, Papa, but I fight like a Russian Cossack. I am just like Aunt Alexandria."

"*Da* but built like your mama. Now we should get some sleep, so I can leave early in the morning. I'll roll out my bedding here in front of the fire." Sending a meaningful glare at Matthew, he continued, "Katarina, you will sleep here with me."

No one contradicted the large man. Certainly, Matthew didn't have the *mykectbo* to do so. There, he was picking up a little more Russian to add to his few other words. He pulled his sleeping bundle out and undressed down to his union suit before sliding in. His last glance was toward Katarina who had an unreadable expression, making him feel lonelier even though they were only feet apart.

Soon he found himself staring at the now-familiar rafters listening to the loud snores emitted from Boris, completely blocking out the soft little breaths he was trying so hard to hear. Tomorrow night would be different. Tomorrow he would be sleeping beside Katarina again. Tomorrow began the end of their time together. He couldn't decide whether he wanted tomorrow to get here or not.

The next day his wrist throbbed, but he carried smaller piles of wood inside after gathering clean snow in buckets to melt in the heat of the stove. Katarina had made a breakfast and extra food for her father to take with him. The sled dogs had shared from the barrel of Aitii's fish and drank the warm water delivered before they were put into harness. Now it was back to the two of them.

"Matthew, is something wrong? You've been so quiet this morning—even after Papa left. I thought it would be like before. That we would enjoy being with one another."

Taking a deep breath, he apologized. "It is, or, at least, it is pretty much. Your father's arrival brought reality back. We won't always be alone. Soon the spring will arrive, and all the trappers will be coming through to trade or on their way to Sitka. I don't want you to end up serving them, working."

"I don't mind."

Pulling her into his arms, he whispered, "No, but I do."

That night, the bedding was placed in front of the stove, the fire built up since it seemed it was getting even colder than before. The rafters were popping with the new freeze, and he stripped down to his long johns and waited for her to do the same. He had spent several hours telling his body there would be no chance of a repeat from the other night or anything resembling it. He thought he had made a pretty good defense of why they should not be more intimate than they already had been.

Katarina came over after turning out the lantern, making her way to him through the shelves and cases of can goods and sacks. Climbing between the furs, they snuggled together as he girded himself to sleep beside her once again—and nothing more. He found a comfortable place to lay his arm next to his head and tried to concentrate on sleep. She was making it impossible with the way her small hand would wind itself in the hair on his chest. How she gave him little kisses across his shoulder. How she snuggled into him placing her leg against his manhood.

"Your father didn't ask for my word, but he implied certain things. I don't feel right about not keeping faith with the intent of our agreement."

"I made no such agreement, so I can do as I wish." She brushed her mouth across one of his nipples which almost had him lifting off the thin mattress.

"Katarina, honey, that needs to stop. I know how I feel, and I know how you feel, but this other, this would be taking things too far. Can't you see I only want what's good for you? You're making it more than difficult to keep you safe."

"My father will be back soon—too soon for my liking. We need to seize the moments we have left. It is like a Russian tragedy, *nyet*?"

"Stop thinking of this like a play, something you can control with words and deeds. This is life, and we need to face the fact you must leave with your father, and I will remain. It has been decided."

"Decided, but not by me. You men think your word is law and women must obey you, but it is a new world out there. Women are making their own decisions, choosing where to live and what to do...taking lovers."

"Katarina, what am I to do with you?"

"I liked what you did with me before only this time I want to feel you inside me, filling me with the manhood I feel pressed up against me at night." She continued to explore his chest with her hands and mouth.

He knew what he should do. He knew what Lorelei would expect of him, but he knew his own weakness and that was to make love with Katarina at least once. He pushed her onto her back so he had more control, could pace his movements, and hopefully keep her safe from an unwanted child.

Covering her mouth with his own, he swallowed her sigh. Her tongue darted out playfully, intriguingly, bringing his own to action as he tasted her thoroughly. He would never get enough of this woman no matter how long she stayed. But he must remember she wasn't for the likes of him. A cowboy from Nebraska in a desolate country and harsh environment.

Her hands framed his face to hold him in place while she leisurely took her time. Kissing and sucking his tongue, teasing him with her own as she arched toward him, pressing her breasts against him. He felt her steer him to the already taut peaks, her nipples firm and ready. Taking first one and then the other into his mouth, he divided his attention between both of them. She was so responsive his erection ached from wanting her.

Stroking her body, he brushed lightly over her mound, feeling her body press into his hand. He allowed himself the pleasure of entering her again, smoothing the way for his throbbing erection. The one that rose to full attention the moment he decided he would give her what she wanted—what he needed.

"Matthew, please...Matthew, you promised."

He hadn't, but he knew what she meant. He led her on, and now wasn't the time to get righteous. She was wound tightly, and he had the key to lessen her ache. He needed to ease her need. "If you're still sure..."

"Matthew, I can't wait to be one with you. Please..." She raised her entire body, pushing toward him, wrapping a leg around him so he couldn't leave her if he tried.

Placing his aroused manhood against her soft opening, he pressed into her, ready to stop if she found the discomfort too much. Her hands found his buttocks, and she pulled him to her widening her legs to give him full access to her female warmth. He felt little resistance, and her hips rose to meet him, her eagerness setting off a male need to possess and be possessed.

Never had he felt so much a man. Never had he felt he filled a woman so well. Never had he felt he was doing the right thing more than at this moment. Her response was everything he could hope for. Her breathing increased to match his deep breaths. His heart pounded in his veins as she met her climax, pushing him over the edge.

He withdrew and spent on her stomach, saving her the burden of a child he would never know about. His breathing returned to normal as he left the warmth of the bedding to find a cloth to wash her off.

As he administered to her need, she asked, "Why did you do that? I wanted the chance to bear your child. Have a part of you with me forever."

"I love the idea of you carrying my child, but only if we are together so I can help you, help our child, give him or her a father. I couldn't let you go if I thought there was a possibility of a child between us."

He saw the tears then came the garbled words. "I knew you couldn't let me go if there was a chance of a child. Now you have ruined my dreams."

He stilled. "Was that the only reason you insisted we make love?"

"No, it's because I love you, and I will use any method to keep you by my side. Telling my father, I may be carrying your child would be the only way to stay together."

"I love that you would face your father and admit to that, but I have obligations here. I was given the chance to own my own business and make something of myself. I think your father will think more of me if I stick this out. Once that's done, I will come for you. If you still feel the same way about me then, I'll fight anyone I need for you to become my wife."

"I am sorry you are so honorable, but one day, as you say, we will be together as we are meant to be."

Although Matthew was trying not to intrude on the father and daughter, he could hear their conversation. "*Malysh*, your Matthew is a good man, a hard worker, but you are a princess. You were not meant to be a cook or washerwoman. Even he agrees with me in this. Love—love you can feel for many people, many times in your life. You will forget this man soon enough once we are back in Russia, back in St. Petersburg."

"But Papa, I know what he is, and he is exactly what I want in life. If it means washing dishes and doing laundry, I will do so. I accept his way of life to be his wife."

"No! The agreement was that you would come home with me." His eyes softened. "*Malysh*, I am an old man and don't have long on this earth. Would you have me live the rest of my life alone and worrying over what might become of you? This life, this land ages one too fast. You deserve to be dressed in silks and satins, diamonds and pearls. You deserve to be dancing in the grandest ballrooms and meeting the richest and greatest of young Russian men."

"I have met and found the man I want to have by my side, Papa. He may not be Russian, but he is the man I have chosen to love."

"*Da*, Katarina, but you cannot listen to your heart alone. Listen to the man you love."

She turned toward Matthew, and he saw the tears. Not stage tears used to get her way with her father, to wrap him around her finger, but true tears, and it tore him up to think he added more pain to her life. He wrapped his arms around her as she moved into them.

"Katarina, my love, we have discussed this and agreed Alaska is not a place for you. This trading post is not a place for you. Your place is with your father wherever that may be. St. Petersburg sounds like a grand place to me, and you should return to the life you were born to have."

Sobs shook her shoulders, and he looked over to the man he hoped would help him say the right things to drive Katarina back to Russia. She would never believe Matthew had changed his mind about loving her. Glancing across the room, Matthew could see the bear of a man surreptitiously wipe a tear from his cheek and realized there would be no more help from that quarter. It would be up to him to convince her to go home.

"Listen, you know about my early life and I tell you truthfully I would do anything, give up anything, to spend a little more time with my pa. He died suddenly without any of us being able to tell him a proper goodbye, to thank him for all he gave up for us, to promise him we would work hard and be grateful for what the good Lord provided. I envy you your father. He may be fit and hearty now, but things change, and you still have the time to spend with him doing all those wonderful things he keeps talking about." He pushed her away from his body so he could stare into her eyes. "You know I love you, but that won't go away. You have the chance I never had to spend time with your father. Take it, grasp it to your heart, hold on for as long as you can."

"Oh Matthew, there is not a man on this earth who

is so loving, so generous, so kind as you. Do you wonder why I love you?"

"I know, and I feel like the luckiest man alive to have found you and spent time with you for as long as we have. If anything, this Alaskan adventure has taught me to follow my instincts. It's how I found a frozen princess of my very own."

She stepped back. "I see you and my father are alike in one way, at least. You are both very stubborn. I will go back to St. Petersburg, but I will not find another man to love because I know I left the best one here in Alaska." Wiping her palms across her wet cheeks, she turned, "Papa, you should get the dogs hitched up while I finish a little packing. I'll come out as soon as I'm ready." She laughed lightly. "I must quit crying first or my eyelids will freeze shut."

As soon as they were alone, Katarina turned to him, holding him in place. "I will wait for you to come for me once your Alaskan adventure is complete. There is more waiting for you in this world and being my husband is only one of them. We don't need to be rich for adventures only willing to try new things. Go new places. Work toward bringing good into the world. I will spend time with my papa, but I will be waiting for you. Do not keep me waiting longer than is needed. We will have adventures together. Marriage will not put an end to our journeys, I can assure you. I can show you much you haven't seen."

"I look forward to that time, Katarina. I will find you no matter where you are in this world if only to say a final goodbye. Live the life you were meant to have."

"I promise you that I will. Just as I promise you, I know we are to be together."

The kiss they shared was a pledge between them. He would no longer lie to himself. Instead, he admitted what he had been denying all along. He belonged to Katarina and she to him. She was part of his Alaskan adventure, but it would not end here.

CHAPTER EIGHT

Watching the rest of his life ride away on a dog sled was the lowest point Matthew ever wanted to be at. All his fine talk about doing what was best for Katarina was going to tear his heart out and leave it on the frozen ground. Inhaling deeply, he returned to the warm cabin and removed every sign Katarina was ever there. Not that he didn't want to remember, but he didn't want the reminders. He didn't need them, and he wanted her things kept for himself. These were things she did and gave to him and they were precious, the only things he would ever have while she had his heart.

He tried to stay too busy to remember the look of sorrow on her face as she pulled the fur up to her nose and waited stoically as her father urged his dogs to take to the trail. Their high-pitched yipping and Boris's deep, bass calls of direction were the last sounds he had of her. He had written a letter to Lorelei. She would read between the lines and commiserate with his loss even from as far away as Nebraska. Boris said he would send it on once they reached Sitka. Matthew didn't know when he'd get an answer. Hopefully, he would be over feeling as if there was a hole in his chest by the time he did.

Two days alone wasn't enough to heal, but Suu and Kimalu returned with furs to tan and meat to stew. Suu showed him the beaver tails she was going to bake and happily took them to the cooking area to prepare them. Matthew was a little worried about trying them, but he hadn't much of an appetite anyway so didn't think it would matter.

Walking past the large cookstove later, he heard a strange pop sound. He stopped and gazed at Suu. "What was that? Rafters freezing again?"

Giggling, she replied, "No, the tails make sounds as they 'pop' open letting steam out."

"I learn something new every day here." He wished he had learned how to forget, or at least ignore, the pain in his chest and the heaviness in his heart. Even without the physical reminders of Katarina, he found himself turning to tell her something or wishing she had seen the sunset or heard the grouse at daybreak. Any little thing would remind him of how much she was missed.

With winter in full-blown fury, Kimalu's younger twin brothers came to stay and help with the hides brought back from the potlatch where whale blubber and meat had been dispersed to those who helped in the hunt. The two, Cumshewa the elder and Guujaaw the younger, brought another team of dogs and large sled which they said Matthew could use to take provisions out to the mining fields.

It was explained to Matthew that when the winter came it was difficult for miners to make it anywhere to buy food and many didn't think of that when purchasing winter stores. They underestimated what they would need to keep themselves alive through the cold dark months. Tedero always took at least one trip out to the fields and even the mining towns which also ran out of supplies when miners found their way to them.

Cumshewa put himself in charge of training Matthew with the dogs since he felt he had the best English.

"You have Aitii, who is mother to several of my dogs and will never let you down. She is the smartest dog I have ever come across, and her offspring come close, thank goodness. I often use her when I am unsure of the terrain."

"I believe that. She saved a person earlier this year by waking me up in the middle of the night so I could bring them inside before they froze."

"She is like that, and she won't allow any other dog to overrule her voice. They all take their orders from her. I think even before they take orders from the musher."

"Wait. Aren't I the musher? I thought I was in charge."

Chucking, the younger man shook his head, "Not when Aitii is with you. She can make the others go the direction she wants, but as I said earlier, she usually knows the best way to go."

As the training began, Cumshewa stood back saying, "Take the handlebow with both hands and get the feel of the sled."

Matthew lifted the sled and was surprised at the weight. "It is much heavier than I thought even without all the provisions loaded."

"Yes, but the dogs pull so that it glides over the snow. They don't lift it but pull low on their bodies to make it follow them. The musher must be careful to make sure the sled stays grounded." Matthew nodded and waited for the next directive.

"I'll explain the dog's rigging, which is one of the

most important things for you to know. That and the positions for each dog within a team. It is important that you hook them up in the right sequence, or there can be problems that will last between the dogs all day."

Laughing, Matthew said, "You mean like there's a pecking order?" Seeing the other man's blank expression, Matthew explained, "When you have chickens, there are certain chickens that get to eat first or enter the yard first, and then their offspring are next. The last chicken allowed in without being pecked on is the low man on the totem pole."

"Totem pole? Like my people carve?"

Realizing his major error, Matthew retraced his thoughts. "It means that certain chickens are not as important as others and their children carry the same place within the, um, chicken community."

Nodding as if he understood, Cumshewa agreed. "Yes, like Aitii's offspring are always more important on a team then some of the others. They are the strongest and smartest, but, also, there is something else. Like in wolf packs. The pack leader's mate and their offspring are fed first after the hunters have eaten."

Matthew nodded and thought Cumshewa had come up with a much better example of pecking order than he had about chickens which seemed few and far between in Alaska.

Picking up the leather straps and leads, he tried to separate them so that Matthew could see each piece. "This is all considered tack, harnesses for the dogs. We take the gangline, which ties the dogs to the sled, and then the three-foot-long tugline, which attaches to the harness then the neckline goes from the dog's collar and the gangline. See, it's about ten to twelve inches long and keeps the dogs going in a forward direction."

Matthew understood the concept but was worried anyway. "Will I need to remember the names, or will it be enough to hook them up properly each time?"

The other man smiled knowing he was giving the information very quickly to see how Matthew picked up on things, but continued, "Use the heavy stakeout chains to keep the team where you want them. It is best, as I said before, to keep the teams separate and sometimes even dogs within a team separate. I have two brothers, Duke and Bleu, who will tear into one another if I allow them too close to each other. As part of a sled team, they both do their job as they should. I suppose it is like Guujaaw and me. There are days we would rather fight than anything else."

Matthew figured he could hook the team up. It was keeping the dogs in order that would be the problem. Not only were many of the dogs siblings, they also looked alike to him. Being sure to keep them straight was making him sweat. Especially after Cumshewa explained how important it was to keep certain dogs separate from others. The last thing he needed was to get between two dogs wanting to tear one another apart. Matthew was kind of fond of his fingers and arms.

Feeding them began each morning with heating water so it wouldn't freeze as it hit the metal water pan. Each dog had their own and each was given a frozen fish. There was a way to do that properly, also, since some dogs naturally needed more fish than others and it didn't have to do with the dog's size. Another thing Matthew had to learn, but it had the secondary effect of having him learn which dog was which. Learning them as he went down the stakeout chain watering and feeding them, Matthew said their names and made them used to his voice. They needed to know he fed them and that when he gave them orders as the musher, they would follow them—willingly.

Matthew finally felt it was time to take the team and sled out for a solo run. He was sweating beneath his parka as the whole family came outside to see him go from hitching up the team to taking them on a run, returning, and then unhitching them and putting them back on the stakeout chain.

He had been out with Cumshewa and, at other times, Guujaaw with both teams, but this was the first time he would be on his own. The sled was empty, which actually made it more difficult to handle, but he wanted to make sure the dogs obeyed him when he was with them alone. He needed to know he could do this. It was important for his business and for his own personal experience.

He had spent his life working on the backs of horses rounding up cattle, but this was a completely different animal. Horses were temperamental, but he understood them, cattle were simple animals while dogs seemed to be always trying to outsmart you. They had a pack mentality but were also competitive with one another and he thought often with the musher. He often thought it was him against them at times. Dogs being man's best friend didn't originate with these sled dogs.

Nervous to have his first time on a sled as the lone human witnessed by all his friends and the only other humans he saw on a regular basis, he bit his bottom lip, hoping the dogs would take pity on him. When he got at the back of the sled and called out for the dogs to move forward and nothing happened, his worse fears were met. Using the whistle, he again remained in place.

Calling one more time, he snapped the whip over the dogs' heads which caused the lead dog to leap forward, and all the others did as well, barking in their excitement to be running. Matthew thought he was going to be dragged behind in an embarrassing display.

"Pedal! Pedal, Matthew, to help keep the sled going." The last thing he saw was both brothers laughing so hard they were bending over holding their stomachs. He hoped he hadn't lost all their respect. If he could get these dogs under control, he could possibly save face yet. He merely had to drive the sled a few miles to tire the dogs out, turn it around, and return, then unhitch the team and never take out a sled again.

It was more difficult than he thought. The dogs could sense his inexperience and his indecision of where he wanted to go. Finally, he knew if he didn't let the animals know who was in charge, they would ignore him and go where the lead dog took them. That was Aitii, which meant she would take him back to the trading post, but not because he told her to. Stopping the dogs, he put the lock on and thought things through.

He was smarter than a dog, even a pack of dogs. He was bigger than a dog, and he was going to let them know he was in charge without resorting to inflicting pain on any of them. He walked the line, checking the hitch line on each of them and talking with them as he did so. Then he went to Aitii to ruffle her neck fur and speak with her.

"Come on, girl, haven't we become friends? Haven't I been good to you ever since you brought Katarina in from the cold? Haven't I thanked you every day for saving her and making me a happy man? The two of us would never have met without your help, and I appreciate it, even if she and I had to separate so soon. You understand, don't you? How much I love her and want to prove myself to her and her father? Make myself a man worthy of her—or at least more of an equal. It will take years, but it is all I have to hold on to for now. Should we show these youngsters how it's done, girl?"

Her yipping and dancing around near his feet buoyed his spirits. Returning to the sled, he lifted the brake and made a piercing whistle which brought on the wagging of tails and the barking of the team as they lurched into motion. He soon saw the top of the trading post coming into view and knew he had been accepted by his team. He would take both teams out a few times before making the trip into the interior.

"You will need coffee beans. Many sacks coffee beans." Matthew laughed, since Suu had been saying the same about almost everything he had put in the pile to take with him on his trip to the mining camps.

Cumshewa brought over a couple of dozen boxes of ammunition and placed them alongside the sacks already piling up. By the time they were finished getting everything, Matthew looked around at his seriously depleted stock. "Are you sure we'll need all this?" he asked the others, looking for their experienced input.

Kimalu nodded. "Matthew, this pile will be gone within a couple of weeks, less if you make it as far as Miller's Creek. Tedero used to do this twice a winter until spring broke. I will restock the trading post so there will be enough here when the fur traders bring in their wares this spring."

"I'm glad Cumshewa is going with me on this trip. It doubles the inventory we can take with us, and he will show me the best trails to take to the biggest mining areas." Matthew was ready for the meal Suu had prepared for them. They would be leaving in the morning with the two sleds and dog teams Matthew had practiced with. "I can't tell you how much I appreciate all of your help." He held up his cup of coffee as if toasting the family sitting there with him.

"Tedero would expect nothing less from us, Matthew. You have embraced Alaska and made it your home. We have embraced you and made you part of our family just as Tedero had been. For as long as you are here, we will be one big family," the patriarch, Kimalu said, as the rest nodded their agreement.

Nodding, unable to word his thanks for their acceptance, he took a long drink from his cup. He was beginning to look on this family as an extension of his own even though he still missed his own brothers and Lorelei this past holiday. Here, he hardly noticed it sliding by with all the preparations going on to learn mushing and readying himself for the long weeks away from his store.

The next morning, Cumshewa and Matthew finished loading the sleds and accepting a few things Suu had prepared for them to eat the next couple of days. "Keep the mash near your body." She instructed him as she patted his midriff. The starter for the sourdough bread they would bake on their trip was already fermenting in a greased, cloth bag next to his skin. He was getting used to the odor it sent off whenever he moved his parka since he had practiced carrying this on him as he drove the dogs the past few days as well.

"Mush!" called out Cumshewa, as Matthew whistled and both teams set off with the other man taking the lead. At least until they made their way to a more used trail Matthew could follow without his guide. Heading into the interior following the summer trail the miners and trappers had used to reach the trading post and the trail back to the village on the lake and then to Sitka.

Matthew wondered if he would ever take that trail to Katarina's direction again. Would he ever earn enough to go to Katarina's father and tell him he was worth his daughter's hand? That he could support her in the manner he had difficulty even imagining. A few things Katarina had mentioned, her travels, her homes, were something out of a fairytale to Matthew. Mystical castles and palaces where the czar, like a king, lived along with various members of his close family which included Katarina and her father.

A problem he hadn't thought about this trip was the time he would have to think. At the trading post, there was always things to do. Help getting wood dried and cut for next year, helping with the hide processing, learning and grading the furs, moving snow out of their everyday paths to the outbuildings and where the dogs were staked out. Every morning, he knew there would be people to speak with and things to do that kept his mind off the family he left in Nebraska and the young woman who left him to return to St. Petersburg.

Now that he had learned the tricks to being a musher, he had time to think—and worry. He needed more work and less time to think of how long it would be before he saw those he loved again. His nephew, his brothers, although thinking of Lorelei was easier. The love he felt for Katarina was so much stronger than the feelings he thought he had about his brother's wife. Now he understood what his sister-in-law had been telling him. That he would find a woman who would move him so much more. Who would take up so much more of his heart? He should write Lorelei and let her know she had been right. Just as she'd been right about so many other things. That he was destined to do something other than help his older brother run the ranch and the family. That there was more to him than what he had tried to do so far in his life.

Cumshewa waved to bring the sled up to his side where the trail widened, and he placed the brake on as the dogs, still with too much energy and excitement jumped toward one another in playful attacks.

"We will cross a river soon, so I will take the team across while you wait and do so after me. It should hold us both, but I do not like to take that chance. If the water is moving quickly underneath or has warmed for some reason, the ice will be thin."

"I understand. Should I wait here?"

"I will wave once I'm on the other side so then you follow where I went. Try to stay within my marks. If you see the snow darken then that is sign there is water on top of the ice coming from beneath. You are to go to the closest land when that happens."

Nodding, Matthew held on to his dogs as the other team bounded away. His whole team jumped and whined, wanting to keep up with the others, but Matthew tried to sooth them with talk while watching Cumshewa closely. They had talked about river crossings, but until you came to one, no one knew what they would feel. He was anxious to see his friend's sled safely on the other side. Cumshewa waved as his dogs pranced in place as he waited for Matthew and his team to cross.

The two drove late into the evening since the moon allowed them to see the wide trail where others had been through since the snow fell. Matthew wondered who else would be out and about in this weather but wouldn't worry it was another trader. Kimalu made it clear that Tedero had been the only man motivated enough to leave his warm trading post simply to sell to miners too lazy or too controlled by gold fever to leave their sites, even for food.

They made camp in the dark with the dogs attached to a snow hook, keeping the dogs close together in one place. He knew they needed to be able to move and fight off any attacking wolves during the night. Otherwise, they would be sitting ducks. He fed the dogs a frozen fish each while Cumshewa started the fire, setting pans of snow on the trivet to heat for water. Matthew was glad to see a pot of coffee added to that as well.

Cumshewa explained they would sleep next to their sleds or even on them under a pile of furs covering the supplies brought along for that purpose. That and they kept the provisions dry. Right now, Matthew thought it best not to lay on the snow and made ready to try to sleep on the lumpy bags of beans and rice. Dinner was the last of the prepared food Suu had sent with them. It seemed they ate every time they stopped, and Matthew still found himself hungry. No one explained how mushing made a man hungrier than a day of chopping wood.

The next day, they came upon a wide river still flowing freely as miners stood almost boot high half in and half out of the cold moving water. Some men came out of their tents as they heard the dogs come to a stop near the clearing where trees had been chopped down for the firewood or poles to make their tents with. Most living quarters appeared to be merely canvas laid over bent branches and sticks. Some had hides laid over the canvas to hold the heat in and the cold and snow out. Small fires put off little heat and much smoke as they fought to stay alive in the falling snow.

Matthew walked toward them saying, "We're travelling through with some provisions if anyone wants to buy something. I've got foods and ammunitions and will take furs and gold in trade." There was mumbling, and Matthew felt sweat trickle down his warm back as a man strode forward.

The man, no older than himself, asked, "Got a knife of any sorts, in there? I broke the blade on mine and can't go the rest of winter without one."

Matthew was glad of the suggestion from Kimalu since the more experienced man had mentioned the need for some tools and hardware. "I have two to choose from if you like. More back at my trading post in *Zvezda Moya*, but both are sharp and sturdy."

"Damn cans. I was trying to open them as they was froze so thought I should eat them afore they went bad. My knife couldn't take the work." He looked at the two knives Matthew pulled out from a canvas wrapping and felt the longest blade with his thumb.

"How much?"

"They go for six bits at the post. How 'bout an

even dollar since I'm delivering and saving you a trip into a town?"

The man nodded and reached for his pocket, pulling out a small leather pouch. Matthew wouldn't have been surprised to see gold flakes or nuggets, but the man had a coin, and Matthew accepted it easily. "Anything I can do for you? I don't have any can goods since, as you pointed out, they freeze this time of year. I have dried beans and rice, though."

"Got any coffee beans? I've run out and thought I could go without, but it's funny how something becomes a big part of your day." The miner was trying to read the bags to know what all was now revealed on the sled.

"I'll take some of those coffee beans as well as long as they ain't too dear." Another scruffy miner stepped closer becoming part of the small group warming up to having Matthew in their midst.

"How's twenty cents? I've got some mixed with chicory for half that if you like."

"Sure, give me that one. I was raised on chicory, so it tastes like home to me. And some of those white beans. You selling them by the pound?"

"Yup, got a pot for me to scoop them into or I have small sacks here…"

"No, I'll get a pot then I can keep the varmints out of them easier. They'll chew right through the cloth otherwise once they come up out of hibernation. I'm about to catch me a few to eat. Some say they aren't bad tastin'."

Chuckling, Matthew had to admit, "Not sure how they taste, but I do have some caribou, bacon, and moose fat for cooking. Seal oil and frozen fish, plus some whale blubber." He named off the items Kimalu and Suu had brought back with them from further north a few weeks ago.

Soon there were numerous men crowding around the sleds asking for what they wanted and taking some of what Matthew could provide. He made mental notes of what the men asked for, but he didn't have, so that next time he would add it to his provisions before he set off. He noticed Cumshewa told the men what he had in his sled but didn't go through any of the items allowing Matthew to set the price and divvy out the purchases.

Later, as they set up their evening camp, Matthew asked his friend about his actions in dealing with the miners.

"I have found that many of those men have problems with dealing with us here in Alaska. Too many remember the wars with their Indians and think we are alike in that way. Our tribes always fought, always took slaves, always hunted, and moved around, but the Russians dealt harshly with us as is the federal government in some portions. My father decided to move with the changes and accept the new way of life. He made sure I learned languages to help me keep up with Alaska's changing ways."

"I can imagine what you have had to give up to remain living in the land you were born to." Matthew remembered how much the American Plaines Indians were losing. How they had to move to reservations or be burned out of their villages by soldiers. How the bison no longer roamed in large herds and railroad tracks crisscrossed the land instead.

"The old way we thought was good, but we spent much of our time and strength fighting. Now we have a common enemy, but the old hurts are still there, and we have decided it is better to change or lose our way of life completely. Perhaps our lives completely."

"I compliment you on your ability to speak English so well. My Russian isn't very much improved, even with your help."

"I spent my early years in a missionary school for us. They wanted all of the indigenous tribes to give up our ways and become like them. I was there almost to manhood but always went to visit my family every summer. The missionaries didn't approve, but what could they do? I knew who and where my family was, and I would simply leave. They weren't bad to me, but they did not understand how strong our lives are tied to the sea and the animals that live there. They are farmers in a land that is not favorable to farmers."

"I can see where there could be clashes. The Indian tribes in Nebraska are to report to their reservation, but its hundreds of miles away. Not within their own lands they have always hunted and lived on, but alongside onetime enemies. Not sure how that's a comfort to anyone."

"I have learned to accept so that I can live the life as I have always known it to be. Hunt when the seals come to land, harvest what the sea and land provide. It is our way and hopefully one my children will enjoy as well, as long as me and my people do not fight progress as those in control think of their way."

"I can't say the way I live is better than yours. It's simply how it is and I'm damn glad I never had to kill anyone to get it that way." The two young men fixed a meal and slept on the sleds after caring for the dogs. In the morning, they prepared to continue further into the bush searching for miners who needed what Matthew had to sell.

On the trail, the two teams kept a few yards apart to make sure that at least one was safely on land if the other went through the uncertain frozen ice. Matthew had noticed that the temperature was changing, but Cumshewa hadn't called for them to stop or even take a break. They had discussed a place where they would stay for the night before setting out.

The overcast sky and quiet trees had become unusually eerier without any wind knocking the branches together. Instead, he noticed a change in front of his eyes as ice fog, a thick winter fog made of suspended ice particles that leaves the trees and brush coated with ice crystals, was forming everything around them into a magically beautiful landscape. Beautiful, but dangerous.

He knew his running mate had to be aware of what was going on around them, but he seemed intent on pushing his team onward. Cumshewa hadn't even looked back, and Matthew didn't want to get closer to him for fear the man knew something he didn't about the covered terrain they were crossing.

They finally began climbing, and the dogs pulled on their ropes trying to get the still heavy sleds up the incline. Both Matthew and Cumshewa had been pedaling then running behind their sleds urging the now tiring dogs on. They finally climbed enough that the ice fog was left behind, and the front team pulled to one side of the open trail to rest.

Pulling his parka down from his head, Cumshewa said, "I'm glad you could keep up. I didn't want to get caught in that fog like that. It becomes difficult to see where you are going, and it can come in and settle in the low areas for hours. I wouldn't want to try to have you follow me if we couldn't get away from it."

"I wasn't sure what your plans were, but I trust your knowledge and instincts when it comes to things like this. It's the first time I've seen ice fog, and it is almost mystical with the crystals glittering in the sun's rays. I don't suppose having it melt and turning to ice on the trail is a good thing, though."

"No, ice fog has taken many lives, and I hoped going higher would work to our favor. I knew the trail rose through here. I still don't wish to stop on such an incline, so are you ready to continue?"

"Yes, lead on. I'm the student here, and I appreciate every chance I get to learn about something new." The front team took off and Matthew counted his minute away before mushing his team into action as well.

A tent camp came into view next to a river as it meandered through the outcropping rocks. Cumshewa put up his hand to stop the sleds from continuing on. "I have heard of this place. It is considered a boomtown, but only has the one wooden structure on what is called the main street. It has no store but does have a casino and saloon in the building with prostitutes above. The other tents probably hold the laundry, restaurant, and miner's living quarters. Do you want to start at the casino?"

Shaking his head, Matthew said, "No, they'll just tack on more costs for the miners. I'd rather sell directly to the user. Might keep some man from dying before spring gets here. We don't have that much left, but I think this will be our last stop. I'll sell what we have left to the saloon if they want it."

"Sounds good to me. I miss my mother's cooking."

"You miss your brother so you're not fooling me at all. I can't win at those games you taught me, and you're needing Guujaaw's competition to keep you entertained." He joked with his teammate since they had become so close on this extended trip. The two young men may have begun as almost strangers, but after a week together on the trail, they were much closer, almost brothers, and Matthew felt comfortable with Cumshewa now.

"You are getting much better, but I will agree that I miss my whole family. This is the first time I have been away from everyone for this long. In school, I had both Guujaaw and my cousin, Koyah. We still all usually meet up at the hunts."

"Let's get down there and finish with what we came to do. I'm anxious to show off these pelts and furs to your father. I think you and I did a pretty good job of bartering."

Cumshewa nodded and called out to his team to mush as it pulled his sled to the bottom of the ravine and the makeshift town. The men's appearance brought out a few people to look them over. Matthew waved and smiled calling out, "I'm from the *Zvezda Moya* trading post and have a few items left to sell if anyone is interested."

A couple of women came out of one of the smaller tents wearing little more than undergarments. Matthew swallowed hard but kept the smile in place. He wasn't sure if the ladies were selling or buying, but one asked in Russian what he had in way of cooking equipment.

"Well, I've got a good knife left, a Dutch oven, and

a skillet. The cookware has been used, but that means it's all seasoned and ready to go."

The woman laughed, and then in English asked, "You bought Tedero's place?"

Nodding, he admitted, "I won it in a card game, but I think it was rigged. He wanted me to take it over to make sure it kept going. That what he built up would still be here after he was gone."

She laughed. "That sounds like Tedero. He was one of my favorites." She didn't say favorite what, but Matthew liked her right off since she seemed to have a soft spot for his friend and mentor.

"I've got some cornmeal and dried beans left. The coffee's all gone, I'm afraid."

"That is all right. I would kill for some *zavark*. You know, the Russian black tea?" She scratched her armpit and looked over the furs laying on top of the pile on his sled that he had taken in as trade. "I will take the Dutch oven and the knife. Not that I need another cooking knife, but a woman can never be too careful or have too many knives."

Smiling, he said, "I'll throw in the black tea I've got. That will be two dollars, Ma'am."

Her eyes travelled up Matthew from his boots to his hat, but he knew she wasn't seeing much since he was wearing the bulky parka, although the hood was pushed back off his head. "Do you wish to take trade?" she asked, and he knew she was offering him a chance to work off a little of his energy.

The memory of Katarina flashed into his mind and he shook his head. "Sorry, but I've got someone waiting on me."

She shrugged and pulled out a small leather pouch

from between her breasts and searched through to get the two coins. They were still warm from her body, and he slipped them into his pocket quickly before he thought too much about them or their heat. As she walked back to her tent carrying her purchases, men came from upstream to check out what Matthew had left on his sled. The other held only furs that they had bartered for, and it appeared after this last stop they would head home with only the provisions they would need along the way.

"Matthew," Cumshewa said, once the customers left with their purchases, "We should not stay in this camp."

Matthew looked at the sky, seeing it was getting dark, and then where the dogs slept alongside a tent waiting for them. "I don't think anyone would mind. We'll clean up everything in the morning or not have a fire at all…"

"No, that is not why. Didn't you see some of those men watching the gold every time people paid you with flakes? They were figuring out how much you are carrying. We need to leave and make camp far from here. The dogs will warn us of anyone approaching once we are on the trail. I will find us a good hiding spot to camp and then we will feel safe. Most of these men have no way to follow for very far. I've only seen one horse, and he is so scrawny he isn't worth them eating."

Nodding, he listened to his friend, knowing Cumshewa had more experience living among these men and knowing their ways. He would have thought of it himself if they were back in Nebraska. He wouldn't have allowed so many people to know what he was doing and how much money he had with him. After selling cattle, he used to separate the money if he had to carry cash and couldn't get a bank draft.

They packed up the items they moved to get to what they needed and waved as they headed further northeast. The trail was well marked and Matthew trusted Cumshewa to find them a safe place for the night. And he trusted the dogs to alert them to any strangers trying to approach them.

Stopping after an hour of fast traveling, Matthew helped set up the fire as his teammate set about getting the dogs settled. They sat down to a hot meal and to enjoy talking about how well the rest of the trip would turn out if the miners kept buying like the ones they had just sold to did.

"I'm glad I decided to follow Tedero's usual way of taking the provisions to the miners if today is anything to go by. It won't take long to empty these sleds and then return for more."

They both faced the fire covered with the furs and slept deeply.

CHAPTER NINE

Coming over a crest of a hill, Matthew found Cumshewa greeting another sled team coming from the opposite direction, and he could tell the men were friends, which often meant relatives here in Alaska. "Come, Matthew. Come meet my namesake, Cumshewa Small. He is my cousin, along with Koyah, but because he is younger was not taken to the missionary school."

The large man laughed and cuffed Cumshewa with a big bear paw of a gloved hand. "I still speak English as well as the rest of you, and I didn't need to get beaten with a rod to do so."

Cumshewa took his loving punishment with grace and explained, "This one is going to a potlach with friends we both know. Do you think we have time to take a day to visit with them?"

Knowing how much these potlaches meant to the natives and how well they had done so far in selling their items, Matthew smiled and nodded. "Of course. You can have fun with your family, and I'll remain with the sleds. I'll set up a campsite nearby and…"

"No, no, Matthew you must come, too. It is for everyone. Everyone will be there, and we will eat and play games and then eat some more. It will be fun, and you will meet my other cousins and all my aunts and uncles. Even some people not related to me." They all laughed because almost everyone here in Alaska seemed related to one another in some manner.

"I doubt that, my friend, but we will go together, and I will try to keep up with the festivities. Tedero mentioned that I should attend one of those to meet more people, so off we go."

"It isn't far, and we will be back on our way tomorrow morning." Matthew had agreed to the visit since he knew there was usually no alcohol at a traditional potlach, and it was more about family and gift giving. He wasn't sure he understood it all or why the authorities tried to stop them from occurring, but he knew the events were part of the tribes' heritage, and he looked forward to watching Cumshewa enjoy being with his extended family.

They followed the other team and soon found themselves on a well-worn trail leading to a clearing surrounded by tall, straight evergreens. There were several cabins built near one another with small, shuttered windows and chimneys spewing smoke. The entire area between the buildings was filled with people of all ages and teams of dogs set out along the perimeter of the trees. The two cousins separated with Matthew following Cumshewa to tether his team behind the other. Aitii barked and leapt in excitement. She was usually the one he could depend on, sitting sedately while he used the snow hook to attach them to the ground.

"She knows many of the other dogs here, so she is wanting to run, but that would cause havoc even if she is related to most of them."

"Much like you, Cumshewa? Do you wish to run and play with the others?" Matthew teased his friend, knowing the man had noticed the games abounding in the snow-covered clearing.

"I may want to join in some of them. The *nalukataq,* which is that blanket toss we passed, is the first I wish to do. I have been known as the best *nalukataqtuaq*, or blanket dancer, in the family. I know I will beat out any cousin here."

Matthew watched the man on the blanket as he bounced higher and higher in the air depending on those holding the edge of the bearded sealskins sewn together. Laughing, Matthew watched as Cumshewa got in line and he went to the circle of people as they slid over to give him room to hold the edge as well. He got into the motion of tossing the individual into the air as the dancer tried to go the highest as well as do tricks such as summersaults in the air before landing and bouncing upward again.

Everyone was laughing and urging the dancer on, so Matthew made sure he made a lot of noise for Cumshewa when it was his turn. Cumshewa did impress Matthew with the height he could reach, but when everyone began calling for Matthew to jump, he wasn't as lighthearted.

"Oh, I don't know about this. I mean, if I broke a leg, I would be up a creek without a paddle."

Knowing that most of them there wouldn't know what he was saying, Cumshewa clapped him on the shoulder and said, "Oh, no, you must try this. It is fun and no one gets hurt—well, not most of the time."

Matthew went good-naturedly and climbed onto the furs, only to feel like he had onboard ship in high winds. The motion the *naluaqtit* made with their lifts was not easily maneuvered, and he spent most of his time laughing and trying to keep his balance and his dignity knowing he wasn't actually going very high into the air. Not like Cumshewa who must have travelled at least twenty-five feet before coming back down.

The misery was soon over, and he climbed down to much laughter and good wishes from those still holding the blanket urging another one to test their skill. It didn't help his self-confidence that the next in line was a boy of about twelve.

"This way, Matthew. I have one that will not take as much training. The *nalukataq* takes a little practice, but this I think you will conquer."

Trying to look affronted, Matthew asked, "Are you saying that I need practice on the blanket toss?"

"I'm trying not to hurt your feelings by telling you my grandmother could jump higher than you did," Cumshewa said laughing, pushing through the crowds to get to a circle surrounding a man sitting on the ground while holding up the opposite foot. Using only the free hand on the ground, the man springs up and kicks a target with the free foot before landing again in his original starting position. It seemed the higher the target kicked the better the contestant. There was a similar game nearby only the player there jumped off the ground using both feet to kick a suspended object with one foot then land on the floor using that same foot to demonstrate balance. As Cumshewa waited his turn to play, Matthew waved at him motioning he was going to explore what other things were going on.

He found a group of younger children all enthusiastically playing a game that looked as if it could hurt. Two opponents sat across from one another with strings tied to one ear at which they kept pulling until one of them gave up. Sometimes the string would come off, but that didn't seem to indicate a winner. It would merely be replaced by the oldest child overseeing the contest and then it would begin again. Endurance of pain must be the objective and Matthew wondered how well his young brothers would do in such a game.

Recognizing the smell of familiar foods, he wandered toward a fire where a large spider pan, one with feet to hold it up from the embers, sat with sizzling meat frying. The woman cooking smiled at him and speared a couple of pieces holding the stick out to him. He thanked her using what little Haida he knew and chewed on the seal meat, nodding his pleasure to the cook.

There was *quaq*, frozen whale meat, as well and *muktuk*, whale blubber with the skin still on it, being eaten raw. He had never gotten the taste for raw meats or fish so passed on that delicacy and continued to stroll around watching more games of skill and daring. It was kind of like a county fair back home, and everyone seemed to be having a good time.

A man carrying a large, wooden doll-like face which reminded Matthew of the totem poles he had seen on his way out of Sitka. He knew they were special to some of the indigenous peoples, including Kimalu and his family. The man was calling everyone to gather near a large fire being built up away from the cabins. The games were abandoned as people gathered and the man made a long speech which Matthew caught very little of.

Patting him on the back, a smiling Cumshewa sat down next to him on the frozen ground. "Did you see how high I kicked? I won over every other man here."

"I saw and I was impressed, but I noticed you didn't play the ear pulling game." Matthew wanted to tease his friend knowing most of the adults hadn't played at the games with the children.

He gave Matthew a look and then explained what was going on in the group. "The man with the mask is telling everyone how happy the family is to have them present to celebrate the hunting of the whales and the birth of their first grandson. It wouldn't matter what the potlach was being held for. They are always a show of a family's wealth and to enhance their prestige among the other tribal members. See. There are the coppers being passed out now."

"The what?"

"Large plates of beaten copper given as gifts. This whole celebration will revolve around giving gifts to those who attended. To show how rich someone is, they will even burn new items and destroy food. We won't be allowed to leave without accepting a gift. Maybe I will get some *avarraq,* um, whale fluke cut into strips. It is one of my favorites and always eaten first when the whales are parceled out."

Matthew thought his friend was pulling his leg about the gifts given to the guests instead of the other way around. After all, the food had been provided by someone, and there had been much of it consumed by the large crowd. But just as Cumshewa had said, large copper disks were being given out as well as other items. Also, a kayak, a narrow, enclosed canoe, was being laid on top of the now roaring fire along with other household items.

He found himself wanting to stop the wasteful

destruction, but then remembered he was a guest of a guest and remained silent. Who was he to tell these people how to celebrate? Who was he to tell them the right and wrong of anything they chose to do?

There was music and dancing beginning while gifts were still being disbursed as well as more items landing in the bonfire. He felt almost dizzy with everything that was going on as the sun sank behind the mountain tops.

Finally, after watching the dancers, the host, who Matthew had met earlier that day, approached and spoke to him. Matthew nodded and smiled at the young woman next to the man and then his host left. The girl smiled shyly but remained sitting next to Matthew who was at a lost as to what to say. His limited words were mostly greetings, a few store items, and a couple of swear words that Cumshewa and Guujaaw had taught him. Nothing with which to hold a conversation with anyone, especially a pretty young woman.

He spent an hour watching the dancing and smiling at the woman whenever their gazes met. He hoped Cumshewa would return and let the young woman know she needn't stay to keep him company any longer. He would be fine watching everything until Cumshewa became too tired and they both headed back to the sleds which they had left in the woods.

Glad to see Cumshewa returning, Matthew stood and said, "Are you tired enough yet to go back and sleep? It seems some of the others are doing so."

"I am tired, as you say, but who is this?"

"I missed her name, but the host brought her over, and she's been here ever since."

His friend gave him a strange look and spoke to the girl. Then looking at Matthew, he said, "I'm not sure you're going to like what I have to tell you. This is Uki, and she is a gift."

"What do you mean, a gift?" Matthew gazed at the woman and turned back to his friend. "You mean a gift for me? I can't accept a human being as a gift. What are you telling me?"

"Look, it's very rude to refuse a potlach gift. I know you're not used to such things, but the tribes here still have slaves as long as the authorities don't know about them. She's from another tribe and has been part of this family since she was small. Now they have given her to you."

Trying not to sweat, he said quietly, "Cumshewa, I am not comfortable accepting such gift. Can't we simply leave her here?"

"But she is yours. They would merely send her on to you. Possibly make her walk to the trading post." Both men looked at the small, young woman with large doe-shaped eyes and braids, and Matthew rubbed his hand through his hair.

"I guess we'll have to take her with us for now. I'm not happy about this, having to bring her along. Maybe we can leave her at the next town we come to." He glanced at her and knew she realized they were talking about her, but not what they were saying.

"Don't worry, Matthew, I'll take her on my sled. It's the lightest right now anyway."

Now why didn't that offer make Matthew feel any better about being given the girl?

The trip home was so much quicker it seemed. The first night, Uki understood when they stopped that she should gather firewood, start the fire, and help unpack what they needed to make a meal. Matthew and

Cumshewa staked out the dogs and fed them while the snow was being melted and heated for their bowls.

Uki's motions were smooth and sure, as if she was used to living this way and not in a cabin or other lodge. He couldn't help wondering what he should do with her once they returned to the trading post. He wasn't going to keep her, but he wasn't sure he could simply give the young woman her freedom either. Some unscrupulous person could latch onto her once she was near civilization. He wasn't ignorant of all the prostitutes located in the seaports and how they probably got there in the first place.

The moon was climbing in the sky when everything was cleared away, and Uki came back from a trip into the brush and stood next to Matthew's sled where he had laid out his bed for the night. Knowing there wasn't anything else to do, he motioned her between the furs and then climbed in beside her. When he felt her begin to remove her clothes, he placed a hand on her shoulder.

"No. *Nyet.* I don't know if you understand me, but I'm not going to lay with you. Not like that. I belong to another."

She seemed confused at first and then when he turned on to his side away from her, she seemed to relax and exhaled with relief. He wasn't sure what her life had been up till then, but he wasn't going to misuse the girl, and he wasn't going to let anyone else do so. Once he had her in a safe place, then he would let Uki decide how to live the rest of her life. He would make sure she had the ability to choose for herself, though. That much he knew Katarina would expect of him.

They arrived back to *Zvezda Moya* as conquering

heroes. Suu and Kimalu came out of the trading post smiling and calling for Guujaaw as if he couldn't hear the cacophony of the dogs barking happy to be home and the others calling out to one another in joyous reunion.

Guujaaw hugged and slapped his brother on the back, ignoring the fact he was covered with fish scales which showed he hadn't been idle while Matthew and Cumshewa had been on the trail. There were more furs stretched out on the side of the tanning building as well. Other than that, everything looked as it had when they had pulled out.

Uki stayed back, unsure of herself in this new environment within these new people. Matthew wanted her to feel part of things so introduced her. "We'll tell you all about our trip, but right now, I'd like you to welcome Uki. She will be staying with us until I can figure a way to get her safely set up in Copper Harbor or Sitka."

Suu took the young girl under her wing immediately in understanding and began to speak with her quietly as Cumshewa showed off the furs they had bartered for. Kimalu seemed impressed, so Matthew figured they must have gotten as good a deal as he had hoped. He also had to remember he had a heavy leather bag filled with gold and coins as well.

That evening, after a large welcoming meal, the family began placing the sleeping furs and blankets on the floor near the still-hot stove. Thinking back on things, Matthew would never have imagined his life, how he lived now, compared to just a year ago. Living with his brother and new sister-in-law and feeling out of control. Thinking he loved the woman his brother had married when in reality he merely coveted his brother's chance of living an adult life.

After meeting Katarina, knowing what true love felt like, he was struck by the fact he came all this way to find the woman meant for him. If he never saw her again, he would know he had at least had those few precious days with her and she with him. He would always hold out hope that at some time and somewhere they would meet again, and they would be able to have a life together. He had to keep that thought or go mad with the loss of her.

He felt Uki next to his back and smiled wondering what the others thought about him owning a slave. Then wondered how he was to give her the freedom in a land where many would never consider her free.

As they had planned, the next trip would give Guujaaw the opportunity to show his skills at bartering and selecting the right furs. The young man would take the lead since he knew the new route, but Matthew felt much more confident this time. Not only was he used to the dogs and their temperaments, but he was more secure in his own abilities on the trail. He could read the weather and the terrain. He wasn't an expert by any sense of the word, but he could survive and the whole reason for being here in Alaska was to prove he could live on his own without his brother's help and counsel.

The morning they loaded the sleds again, there was one more to say goodbye to. Uki was staying with Suu who told Matthew the young woman was very well taught as to doing both household chores and working with the furs and pelts. The young woman seemed to be happy with her new home and everyone had accepted her into the group. Matthew would worry about taking her to a town once spring came.

Heading in the opposite direction they had the first trip, Guujaaw set a good pace and the teams were off, pulling the loaded sleds easily over the now settled snow. Remembering what was discussed the evening before, Matthew knew this would be the last such trip for the year.

Cumshewa had said, "We must be done travelling when the breakup comes. When the spring thaw occurs and many of the now frozen rivers and lakes are too weak to take a sled across."

Matthew realized spring must be right around the corner and he had to contemplate his next move. He had a summer to go through and then another long winter before he would feel he had enough time into the business to approach Katarina's father and ask for her hand in marriage. Ask that Matthew be given a chance to prove his worth even if he would never match a Russian prince.

There were signs that spring must be close. Not the budding of the trees and bushes, but other signs like more animal tracks in the snow. And less snow although he thought it was as cold as it had always been. They had easily found several mining areas newly set up that fall by the looks of things. The rivers still flowed freely from the mountain runoffs, but most were using placer mines, those areas dug into the permafrost using pick and shovels and pure grunt work by those wielding them. He had never seen men so decrepit and in need. Guujaaw did much of the bartering which was probably a good thing or else Matthew might have simply given the men who appeared to be starving the items they needed.

The gold kept piling onto the scale, so paying hadn't been an issue. It must be as Kimalu had explained. The men didn't want to leave a good claim in case someone came along and started mining it for themselves. At this rate, they would be sold out of foodstuff and be ready for the trip back. They had even sold the two picks he had brought along on this trip. The permafrost was harder than the metal being used to mine it and tools were needed or no work could be done.

They were going to travel to one more site before calling it done. Guujaaw said he knew of a place further up the mountain, although it was still easily accessed by sled. As became their way, the first sled went across the river and then waited for the other. Matthew was in the lead and had conversed with his friend to decide the best spot to cross since they knew further down the mountainside the river ran to open water. Here, it was frozen, and after testing the ice closest to the bank, Matthew got onto the sled and called out for the dogs to, "Mush!"

The river flattened out here and the banks not steep, indicating the water usually didn't rush through this spot but the dogs, especially Aitii, began to pull to the left, ignoring his call for her to remain true. To pull straight up the other side.

Then he heard it between the harness clinking and dog's panting. The sound of deep thunder. He looked up to see the same gray sky that had been with them for the past few days and then thought he heard it again. The dark spots, following a jagged line in the snow covering the ice, seemed to appear from nowhere. How had that happened when he had just looked there? How had those spots gotten so much larger since his first glance a moment ago?

Guujaaw's shouting from the shore made him realize what he heard and what he was seeing. The ice was cracking beneath the sled's weight and the dark spots was water coming up through the ice. The ice which was now cracking, allowing the river water to seep up and weaken the rest of the ice supporting him.

He called out for Aitii to go faster, realizing speed was the only thing that would save them, save the team as they pulled the sled to the bank. Stepping off the sled, he hoped the dogs could pull themselves and the sled to safety while he held on and ran behind. He didn't want to be left on the melting ice, possibly be left on an ice floe, but he didn't want his weight to hold the dogs back either. Not sure if he had made a good decision, he wouldn't let go of the sled, thinking they all could make it to shore before the ice gave way completely.

Hearing Guujaaw shouting and waving from the shore, Matthew held on tightly, praying that he had done the right thing. Lessen the weight on the sled while remaining with it and the team. He seemed to remember being told he was safest with the dogs. Safest putting his faith in Aitii. The barking and yipping from both teams filled the air as everyone was aware of the danger and seemed to be egging one another on. Urging that everyone use all their strength to pull or push the sled and its members forward.

Feeling the brush of branches against his sides as the sled was pulled further, Matthew sighed and released his hold, having only become wet from the knees down where he had been dragged through the now open water behind him. Waving to Guujaaw who waited worriedly on the other side, his friend shouted something and then took his team further upstream. Matthew lay for a few minutes savoring the hard, snow-covered permafrost beneath him and saw that Aitii had stopped the team's progress and was sitting waiting for his next command.

Realizing he needed to get warmer, or at least keep his legs from freezing in the now wet leggings he was wearing, he struggled out of them along with his mukluks which were filled with water. Climbing under the furs on the sled was his only option as he hoped he could keep his body temperature high enough to stay awake. Having taken care of Katarina, he knew that was the biggest worry right now.

Aitii jumped and whined and then he felt her weight on top of him as he shivered trying to get his body warmer. She licked his face until he had to cover it beneath the furs as well, but she wouldn't get off him remaining on top for what seemed like hours. He couldn't be sure though since time seemed to be either racing by or dragging slowly. Realizing he might be hallucinating, he tried to do what needed to be done. He remained where he was under the furs, curled up into a fetal position while hoping he could feel his own feet which were ice cold. But at least he felt them—or at least he thought he did.

"Matthew, Matthew. Are you still alive?" The voice of his friend brought him from a sleep he had been fighting, knowing it wasn't good to fall asleep after becoming cold and wet as he had just done.

He felt Aitii jump off him and peeked out to see Guujaaw's worried face not three inches from his. The man leaned back laughing. "I thought you were a goner. It took me so long to find a safe place to cross. We will have to find another way when we head back home."

"I'm going to stay on this side until spring comes and the water warms up."

Laughing, Guujaaw shook his head. "We will want to head for home much sooner, I think. Don't worry, I will take us to a place to build a fire and get your things dried out properly."

Matthew hated to put the extra work on the man but knew he was safest under the furs. He felt his sled being pulled further uphill and then left on a flat area. The other dogs were nearby, and the teams greeted one another noisily as they always did. He stayed beneath the furs, even as he was handed a cup of hot coffee, glad he hadn't sold all the bags of beans yet.

"Matthew, are you all right in there? Are your feet warming up?"

"I think I'm fine, Guujaaw. No need for you to become a heater for my frozen body. I know what that's like, and it isn't pleasant. Like hugging a block of ice."

"Yes, but it is the polite thing to offer. I am glad there is plenty of dry wood here and the fire is really quite large. Your mukluks will be dry by morning and then we will continue. Unless you wish to return to the trading post?"

"No, I want to finish our trip. We don't have that much left, and I want this trip to be as successful as the first. A little cold water isn't going to stop me from doing the same a Tedero always did."

"I agree, but then it is not my feet which got wet and cold." He heard the other man move things around and the sound of another pan scraping metal. "I may as well take advantage of this fire in more than one way. I will make a full meal with extras to pack for the rest of the trip. The mining area I know of is not far from here, and we can make camp nearby for a day or two. I trust the men there not to come after your gold in the night."

The last stop was a camp with actual wood cabins and several paths leading further up into the mountains. A large man came striding toward them as soon as the sleds pulled into what might be considered the center of things.

"Ah, Guujaaw, it is you, but this is not Cumshewa. I can tell even if it is that man's team."

"Yes, Ivan, he is the new owner of *Zvezda Moya,* and my brothers and I have been working with him this winter." Turning to the burly blond-haired man, he continued, "You are the last stop before we head back. We do not want to be on the trails during the spring breakup when the rivers will rush too quickly with the new melting snows."

"I almost gave up hope of seeing anyone. I heard of Tedero's troubles. I will miss him. He was a good friend to me. Gave me food on credit. Did I ever tell you that? But I paid him back, and we have been friends ever since," Ivan smiled, remembering Tedero as many had along the trail and at each stop.

Nodding, Guujaaw said, "It was the same for my older brother. The seals did not come one year, and Kimalu and his wife stayed with Tedero for months until more food could be found. Tedero never asked for a penny, but he understood the Alaskan way. How we must help others at times." Then waving Matthew over, he introduced them. "This is Matthew, who now has possession of the trading post. Matthew, this is Ivan the

Brave. He is called that because he once backed down a bear wanting to attack the campsite." The man put out his large, calloused hand to shake Matthew's.

Ivan laughed heartily, reminding Matthew of his friend Tedero. He could see where those two men would be very good friends. Of a similar size, they seemed to be cut from the same cloth. Both Russian immigrants who stayed on after the sale to the United States. Both men sure of their place in the world and comfortable with the world around them. Matthew wished he had that as well.

Half listening to the two other men, Matthew felt divided. He didn't want to go home, exactly, but he wanted to make sure home was still safe and secure for everyone living there. He wanted his brothers their wives and children all safe and happy. And he wished the people back at *Zvezda Moya* the same thing. He wanted them to prosper and be free to hunt and live the lives they had always lived. And he wanted to find Katarina and if not have her for his own at least know she was happy with her choice. Happy without him.

The two others walked toward the largest cabin and Matthew followed. Ivan turned toward him, "Come and tell me how it was between you and Tedero. I saw him before he left, but he said nothing of being sick. That was new to me to hear that. I wanted to punch my old friend for being so secretive, but then what could I have done? Heh? Tedero lived his own life just as he wanted, but some of us would have liked to have known it was the last time we would be seeing him. I don't know. Maybe it is better not to remember tears. Maybe it is better to remember him beating me at cards and then leaving, laughing, saying he would let me win next time."

"I have a funny story about playing cards with Tedero I will tell you tonight after supper," Matthew said, remembering his friend more this trip than at any other time. Possibly the fact it had been almost a year since his arriving in Alaska and his meeting Tedero on ship. Possibly it was the anniversary that was making him so morose about his friend. That and running into more people who knew the man. More memories told to him of the man he knew for such a short time, yet had made such a difference in Matthew's life.

That night the vodka came out. The memories and the laughter followed by tears which is the way of the Russians, Ivan told them all as they sat around the fireplace in the cabin. It seemed to have been there for several years, but Matthew didn't ask. It wasn't his place to question as to why a man stays mining in an area that wasn't paying out much. No one seemed to be making much money, although they had bought all that he had left on his sled.

"Tell me about the bear, Ivan. I have seen them far off when I first got here, but not one up close. Don't think I've been near one of their caves or anything either."

Laughing like Tedero used to do, Ivan said, "You will smell him before you see him, my friend. If a bear wants a place to be his own, he marks it with a smell no one could forget."

Guujaaw nodded with a smile, as if he too had come across the odor himself.

"Like deer, you mean?" Matthew asked them.

"Like nothing you have ever come across, I mean," Ivan repeated. "Anyway, I was mining beside the river, minding my own business, and all of a sudden, there was a roar behind me. I could smell his breath and feel it against the skin on my face he was so close."

Matthew liked the way Russian's told you a story. It was always bigger, more dangerous, louder, and this one smellier than anyone else's. He nestled back into the furs he had brought in from the sled to listen and enjoy.

"I didn't want to leave since I had just found a very good area of nuggets. As you may know, shallow placer mines are where we chip out gold from the topsoil here. Small bits and flakes. Everything is kept and when added together makes it worth the time. But I had found nuggets. Those have been left by the great glaciers as they scraped mother earth centuries ago. Eons ago. That gold may have been brought from other lands even from the California gold areas…"

"But the bear didn't want your gold nuggets." Matthew dared interrupt the story, as Ivan probably had wanted him to do. As Tedero would always tell a story wanting to get the person to whom he was telling the story to become involved in the whole experience. Feel a part of the excitement or fear.

"No, I think he thought I was there to hunt his salmon. The large fish had been coming upstream to spawn, and the bears had been feeding on them for weeks. Unfortunately, where I had set up my claim was exactly where this bear had been fishing. Where he had marked the territory as his and anyone with any sense would have kept away. But I was young and untrained and didn't understand what the odor I had kept smelling meant. It meant I should be moving on. Not staking a claim on someone else's spot."

Knowing he wasn't expected or needed to keep the story going, Matthew waited as Ivan drank down a glass of clear liquid before continuing.

"I had already pulled out several good-sized nuggets, when I saw one the size of an acorn. Really! That large and pure Alaskan gold is of higher grade than anywhere else in the world. Not mixed with lesser metals like in the United States. No, these were good Alaskan nuggets, and I wasn't about to allow a bear to chase me away from it. If I left then, it may have washed further downstream, or I wouldn't find the exact spot again. I had nothing marking that portion of the river and so I stood to fight for it. I had as much right to that section of the stream as he did."

He saw Guujaaw as entranced in the story as Matthew was. Smiling at his friend, he knew it wasn't the first time the story had been heard by him. Knowing that this story was probably told every time the two men met up and each time it altered a little. Each time, something became larger, more dangerous, or funnier. Although Matthew couldn't figure out how the Russian could make this one funnier since bears were very territorial. At least Ivan had made it out of the confrontation alive so there was a good ending in there somewhere.

Making sure he had both his audience's attention, Ivan told them with lowered voice, "I stood up as tall as possible and lifted my hands wide into the air and roared as loud as I could. I had no weapon or even a stick close by to wave or hit upon the ground. I had only myself and I had to make the bear know I was as serious about keeping that area of the river to myself as he was."

Unable to keep quiet any longer, Guujaaw said, "And he ran away because he wasn't going to fight you when there were miles of river for him to choose from." Laughing, Matthew's young friend added, "I like this ending almost as much as the one where you toss a salmon at the bear and he took it as payment for the river bank."

"Aw, now you have told Matthew one of my favorites. I will need to find another bear story to entertain him when he comes again next winter." He reached out to add another cut log onto the fire, and the flames flared, showing long claw marks starting at the man's wrists and going up his arm. He knew Matthew had seen the scars and shrugged. "Sometimes I win, and sometimes the bear wins. We can only play the hand we are dealt."

Following the other two men's movements, Matthew pulled the fur around his neck and went to sleep, wondering at a man's ability to turn a near-death experience into a funny story to entertain guests. He wondered if when he had been in Alaska as long as Ivan had, if he too would have a funny story. Like of how he crossed a river and fell through the ice but lived to tell about it. He didn't have the scars to lend credit to it, but he thought, given enough time, his story could be as entertaining.

CHAPTER TEN

The trading post became busier as spring arrived, and the trappers came through making their way to Sitka to sell their winter harvest or traded with Matthew for food and needed items. Kimalu helped with the furs while Suu translated many of the languages unfamiliar to Matthew. He was glad he was busy. Kimalu made a monthly trip to Sitka to trade in the furs the business had and order more provisions to sell. It was working as smoothly as Tedero had promised. Everything should have seemed idyllic. All except his memory of a beautiful violet-eyed princess who left with his heart.

And it didn't help that Uki and Cumshewa were now sharing their furs and by the sounds of things each night more than that. Not that Matthew resented them their time together or the growing love he could see was there, but it made him wish for the same for himself and Katarina. Made him regret being the man he was and not the man he needed to be to claim her as his. He was prosperous, but not that prosperous. Not enough to go to Katarina's father and ask for her hand. To have her live the kind of life her father provided her with. The kind of life a husband she could have in Russian could provide.

The couple finally said they would be getting married when the next potlach occurred within the family. Then all the relatives could meet Uki and wish the newlyweds well. Suu and Kimalu seemed happy with the outcome. Matthew thought Guujaaw was happy for his brother, but there was some complaint about the eldest always getting everything first.

Matthew was busy getting the outside of the trading post cleaned up as the winter snows melted. Broken branches littered the ground and the dogs had to be moved to keep them from being left in mudded areas. At least the water didn't have to be heated each morning, since water in buckets kept near the stove was warm enough not to freeze when poured into the bowls. The fish were still frozen, buried in the hillside of permafrost, but the dogs didn't seem to mind.

Thinking about Kimalu's next trip to the coastal port, Matthew wondered whether he should go with him and possibly see his friends he had made there, like the Kashevaroff family. Seeing them would bring memories of Tedero back, but the memory of the Russian seemed to be with Matthew most of the time now. Perhaps it was because the anniversary of their first meeting had come and gone or because Matthew had settled into this new land and learned to love it just as his friend had told him he would.

It would give him some time to look at new items coming in on the ships and perhaps to ask people in the Russian community if they had heard anything about Boris and his daughter. If there had been a marriage in the family...

Why pretend? Especially to himself. He was being driven by the need to know how Katarina was. If she had gotten on with her life or if their meeting one another, if their time together had meant anything to her. Possibly as much as it had to him. In one way, he hoped she had forgotten him or at least admitted the need for her to move on. For her to make a life in her own country with one of her countrymen. He knew her father would select a good man for her. Someone to take care of her and keep her in the style she was raised to live.

Those thoughts took over his thinking for several days, and he had almost decided not to go with Kimalu after all. Why possibly hear that she had married or was even engaged? Not out of his reach exactly, but no closer to being his either. This self-torture wasn't getting anything settled, and he wished there was a way to keep from remembering her and how good she felt in his arms.

Making a decision, he would go to Sitka and see if there was a letter waiting there for him and if not, he would send one to her. Just to tell her that he had made it through his first winter and wishing her well. That shouldn't be anything that would anger her father or a future husband if there was one. Then she could answer him or not, and he wouldn't take it as encouragement if she did. She was a sweet person and would want him to be well with his chosen life as much as he would want the best for her.

Walking toward the dog's food, he noted they were more excited than usual. The sun had been out all day and the buds were beginning to show on the trees. He wondered if there was a way to take them for a run and get this energy used up a little. He could see them wanting to do more than wait and the warm weather must make them antsy just as it was doing to him.

As he reached the door into the earth that kept the cold in and the heat of the spring days out, a shadow fell across him, making the entire hill go into darkness. He glanced behind him and felt the air whoosh out of him. A brown bear was between him and the sun bringing the shadows. Recently out of hibernation, the bear wasn't as large as he would be since the early spring hadn't provided the food he would get later in the year.

Matthew had gotten out of the habit of carrying his rifle with him when he came outside since nothing ever needed shooting before. Now he regretted becoming so complacent. He also regretted not having anything else handy with which to protect himself in case the bear was to attack, and it seemed as if it wanted to attack.

It was now standing on its hind legs making more of a shadow than he had at first. The dogs barking and snarling had gotten louder, at least to Matthew's ears, but everyone was away from the post. They had finally gone to the potlach where the wedding would be held, but since Matthew wasn't a relative, he stayed on to run the post. He had done it alone before, and they would be back in a day or two. Possibly to find his mangled body shredded around the compound.

Thoughts of Ivan's account of fighting off the bear and the welted scars apparent on the man's arms flashed through his mind. Could he actually frighten the bear off by appearing as large as he could and growling? Right now, the real bear was merely huffing his breaths and swaying as if uncertain what to do with this human in front of him. As if unsure how to go about eating him.

Remembering the story brought back the reason for the altercation in the first place. Ivan had been between the bear and his meal. The salmon in the stream.

125

Matthew was in the same position. The bear could smell the dog's fish behind that wooden door and buried within the permafrost. He eased down and tried to open the latch with his hand behind him.

Raising its head, the bear sniffed the air as if able to smell the fish coming within its reach even though the door hadn't come open an inch. Matthew was having trouble with pulling it open from his position but knew it may be the only chance he had. If he could get the door open, he had a small chance of saving his life.

The dogs were going wild, and he could hear Aitii's high whine as she urged the others to higher and higher pitched yelps and whines. Would they tear lose their restraints and attack the bear from behind? Keep its attention on something other than Matthew allowing him to escape and get to the post? Get to the loaded rifle kept just inside the door?

Nothing indicated that was going to happen, although he knew they were trying to get at the bear. It was instinctual in them to fight off the other animal within their territory, so close to their own food.

Expelling his held breath as the latch finally lifted and the door opened as his body leaned forward. The bear's attention was now riveted on Matthew and the open door behind him. Swinging it wide, Matthew reached in quickly then jumped aside, hoping the enticing smell of salmon would take the bear's attention off of him and back to the fish which was probably the bear's original draw to the compound.

With a roar, the bear lumbered toward him, but there wasn't anywhere else to go. Even with the door open to the food source, the animal seemed to resent

Matthew being there and possibly trying to take some of the stored fish. Raising the short-handled pickax that was used to chip the fish apart for the dogs, Matthew stepped into the bear's attack. A large paw swiped toward Matthew as he ducked under it, bringing the pickax up with a loud cry of his own.

The sharp point of the pickax dug into the bear, making it stumble back a couple of feet before Matthew pulled it out and raised it again, aiming for where he thought the animal's heart was. Hoping that he could penetrate the bone and ribs enough to bring the animal to a stop.

It didn't stop, and Matthew pulled the pick back once again fearing that if he tried running the large animal would pull him to the ground and maul him to death. Just as cattle had been taken down and killed by Nebraskan bears.

As he readied himself for another furious blow to the animal's chest, the mammoth animal seemed to teeter and then fell as Matthew jumped out of its way. Trying to catch his own breath, he waited for signs of any movement. Signs the animal was merely taking a rest before rising up again and tearing Matthew's head off. He knew he would be reliving this moment over and over in his nightmares and daydreams. Thoughts of what he could have done or should have done would haunt him. Haunt him until he found a way of telling the story to make other's laugh.

Make his listener picture the half-starved bear looking for a satisfying meal that wasn't juniper berries and termites. Make his listener laugh at the danger since the teller had evidently lived through the altercation, that they had lived to tell about it. He had wondered how men like Ivan could make something so horrific seem trifle and now he knew. No one could explain how one felt or how one accepted fate. How even in an unfair fight, a fight no one would think the man would win over nature, fighting for one's life could change one's opinion of life and everything it ever meant.

Stepping back from the now-quiet carcass, he heard everything once again. Not only the cacophony of the dogs, but the chirping of the starlings flitting among the treetops, the buzz of the little biting black flies that had hatched recently, and the hum of an insect not far away. The head of the animal was huge as he contemplated what to do with it. How to move it and clean up the area. How to simply feed the dogs and calm them so that they didn't get hurt trying to slip their bindings. Living life as he had ten, fifteen minutes ago.

Such a short time to change a man's life. End it or allow him to continue, but Matthew wasn't going to continue as he had once thought. His main concern when he thought he would die was the fact he hadn't fought for her. Fought for Katarina. Promised to come to her as soon as he could. To hell with worrying about what her father thought about him. What he said to him or about him. This wasn't about her father. It was about them. Katarina and Matthew.

What he had and didn't have wouldn't change the man he was or the love he had for Katarina. He wouldn't allow such mundane things to control his life or hers. He would fight and struggle in Alaska to get enough money to go to Russia, find her, and let her tell him whether she would live side by side with him. The love they had for one another would guide their lives, not any one man's vision of what makes life worth living.

Matthew knew what made his life worth living. To be reunited with Katarina.

From the moment he gutted the bear and began tanning the skin, Matthew's primary goal was to find a way to get to Russia, and once there, to get to Katarina. This skin would be part of that goal. Not only had the animal's attack made Matthew realize what was important in life, it was worth a hefty amount since it was in excellent condition, barring a couple of pickax marks in the chest. It had been a young male, so its paws and nails were in good shape as were the teeth. Kimalu and his brothers told Matthew to make a necklace of them and wear it as a talisman to ward off other bear attacks. Matthew laughed, saying, from now on, he would just make sure not to stand between a bear and his dinner.

Then he realized how life-threatening events can end up not only changing a person's thoughts on life and living but also become a humorous outlet for the experienced fear. He had wondered about Ivan's account of the bear attack he had lived through knowing it was and wasn't what he had told them before the fireplace in the small cabin the man made his home. Now he thought about how to tell Katarina and if he would tell her at all.

Although she had told him she loved Alaska and her time spent there, she had never faced an angry bear or had a loved one face one before. She might not find anything funny about the event and worry about returning with him to his adopted land. Perhaps he would tell her after they were married and had lived in Alaska for a few years. Possibly on their thirtieth wedding anniversary. That sounded about right. He could always postpone it if he thought she couldn't handle it at the time.

With the arrival of spring, the number of trappers staying overnight for baths and socializing, increased dramatically. Matthew got out a pick and shovel, heading for the spot he had plenty of time to find. The right place for a privy. The ground facing southeast was as thawed as it was going to get, so putting it off any longer wouldn't get the job done any faster. Like branding. Roll up your sleeves and get er' done.

The sun beat down on his back as he swung the pickax, getting into the permafrost sooner than he thought possible. This may end up a shallow privy but at least it would be one. Answering natures call outside in a full-blown blizzard was something he only wanted to do once. Lifting the pick, he let it fall to the ground, breaking up pieces of frozen dirt which he threw onto a pile near the small wooden shed already built by his own two hands. Again, and again the pick fell, and Matthew began to have more respect for the men who did this sort of work, day in and day out, to make a living at mining. No wonder some gave up before finding the gold promised to them through hard work.

Yep, work hard and reap your reward. The pick landed again but bounced rather than dug into the ground. He moved slightly and wielded the heavy tool again. Again, it failed to move the earth. In Nebraska, that would mean a rock, so he dug around with his hands to see how big a boulder he was dealing with. He hated to think all this work was for nothing if he had to move his privy because of some dumb rock.

His fingers found the edge and worked his hand

around the stone. It wasn't very large, so he kept removing the dirt and used the shovel to pry the stone out of his way only to find another. He continued to dig stones up and toss them aside. This was harder work than he thought it would be as he broke into a sweat, wiping his brow on his sleeve.

The sun, which would be with him over twenty hours a day this time of year, glinted off one of the stones where the shovel nicked it prying it out. It caught his attention and pure curiosity had him picking it up, brushing it off, and weighing it in his hand.

He thought it couldn't be. He thought it wouldn't be. He thought it was too easy to be true. Calling out for Kimalu, he began brushing off the rocks he found while digging, getting more and more excited as stone after stone was made of the same material. Gold. Gold nuggets the size of his fist and larger. Bigger than anything brought to the trading post, bigger than anything he thought gold came in without having melted it down from flakes. But here was nature making the prettiest solid gold rocks heavier than a bar of gold each.

Kimalu came from behind the cabin where he tanned hides and looked at what Matthew was wiping off and piling separately from the dirt. Smiling the older man nodded, "You found gold. Tedero always said this was his lucky gold mine." Then he turned to return to his work.

Tedero had told him Kimalu didn't care about gold but thought riches came by way of furs, whalebone, and seal oil.

Matthew kept digging and kept finding nuggets. Some smaller and some larger but all looking like pure gold. He needed to tell someone. Someone other than Kimalu and Suu who cared even less than her husband had about his find. He placed his gold into a sack and decided to go to Sitka and file a claim or do whatever he needed to do to make this gold his.

His first stop in Sitka was to visit the only man he knew and trusted in the town. Peter Kashevaroff was at home when he arrived. "Ah, Tedero's young friend. Come in, come in. Natolla, come meet Tedero's friend, Matthew. Eh? I got it right, *nyet*? Matthew Foster from Nebraska. How can I help you? Have you, news?"

"I have something I need help with, yes. I'm not sure what I'm supposed to do now."

"Sounds interesting, but I need more information to be of help to you." He led Matthew to the fireplace where a much smaller fire burned this time of year and then probably only because it was used to cook the meals.

As he sat, the inevitable bottle came out while Natolla brought a dish of pickled herring and rich, dark bread. After pouring two glasses of vodka, Peter sat patiently waiting. "I guess I should just show you. You'll probably know by seeing them." He bent down and took out one nugget at a time. He had washed them in the stream and now they looked exactly what they were. Smooth lumpy rocks all shiny and bright. The silence from her husband brought Natolla closer to see what Matthew was taking from the bag.

Peter took a gulp from his glass. "This very good, Matthew, very good. I take it you found these rather than someone paid you with them at the trading post."

"Yes, I found them near my cabin, so what do I do now? Are they mine? Do I need to file a claim? I never thought to ask."

"Well, our friend was very clear that everything he had up there: building, inventory, land, was all meant for you as part of the sale. He would be happy for you, for your good luck."

"And it was purely luck." Knowing he appeared bashful, he admitted, "I found the strike digging a new privy. I couldn't face another winter with my backside hanging out."

The man hid a smile in his bushy beard, saying briskly, "I can get you settled down at the assayers. He will put this in safe for you, or we can open bank account. Eat up, and we will go now. I don't believe in putting off today the claim you can make for tomorrow. Too many slips of the cups to the lips, *nyet*?"

"I agree wholeheartedly—I think. I'm glad for your help."

"Any friend of Tedero's is a friend of mine. You are honorary Russian. I tell you this."

Peter was as good as his word. He cut through red tape and vouched for Matthew's validity in stating the gold came from the site of the trading post. Filings were made as well as bank accounts opened. It all happened so quickly, Matthew was grateful for the Russian's help with it all.

Once they all explored the half-dug privy, the large Russian's son offered to help set up a mining operation and work as the foreman. Matthew trusted Peter and his family, realizing they had been Tedero's friends because that man had trusted them so thoroughly. Everything had been set up to protect Matthew's interest so far, and Peter's son was hired to do what Matthew knew he couldn't do.

A mine operation would be set up since there seemed to be many more nuggets just below the permafrost, possibly deeper, but only digging would tell them where and how much. The amount of gold there to be mined was unfathomable, and Matthew became heady just thinking about it. But there was always something more important than gold on his mind.

Now he was going to prospect for other riches. He was going searching for a princess with violet eyes who held his heart hostage.

CHAPTER ELEVEN

The port of Vladivostok, Russia, spread out in front of him. There was little in way of buildings or even town behind it. What there was, were piles of furs with buyers and sellers bidding over one another to get the best price. Wagons piled high with various furs, sometimes bone and tusks, made their way through the muddy field to what appeared to be muddy roads.

It had been more than a year since he had seen Katarina, almost a year since his life changed while digging a privy. He left his mines, two of them so far, in the very capable and trustworthy hands of Peter's son, Nathaniel. Tedero One and Tedero Two would be sending gold his way for years. Kimalu accepted ownership of the trading post, and Suu cooked and washed clothes for the miners working the site. Nathaniel and his family had a small cabin while a bunkhouse was just finished for the miners to live in. A bunkhouse much like they have in Nebraska.

Now he was free to find Katarina. See if her feelings had changed. If she had married one of those Russians her father planned on throwing at her, possibly talked her into marrying. Matthew wasn't sure what he would do if she had, but he had to see her personally to know her heart. What she needed from him, if anything.

Matthew had a long way to travel to reach St.

Petersburg and if Boris and Katarina were traveling, then he would follow. Money wouldn't be an issue, but time couldn't be bought. Time was limited. Time was his enemy.

Departing the ship with his one valise, he walked towards one of the wagons full of furs. With what Russian he knew and hand gestures, he paid the driver to take him to the ferry landing where Matthew could ride along the rivers and canals with the furs to a city. He travelled through the lakes and rivers northward navigating the central area. From there he would make his way across the continent using the roughly drawn map Peter had given him to follow.

It had been a number of years since Peter was in this part of Russia, so he didn't vouch for the accuracy. Matthew hadn't told his friends why he was travelling to St. Petersburg but let them think he wanted to see Tedero's homeland. His first stop will be Tedero's adopted home town where he was buried next to his wife.

From the ferry, he took a public coach north in the direction he needed to travel. A few questions and he made his way to the Greek Orthodox cemetery with large, important-looking carved stone monuments. Family names marked fenced off areas containing several other headstone markers. Some aged and some newer appearing. For some reason he didn't think he'd find his friend in one of those. He thought of Tedero as being more likely a common man. A working man who made his way up in the world by his own grit and muscles. As he walked further, near the back edge there were more gravesites of less opulence and majesty. That is where he found the gravestone marking the wife's grave with older-looking carved dates and words and then a fresh addition of the year before for the husband's side. This was the last resting place of Tedero, his Alaskan friend. He matched the name with the one printed using the Russian alphabet for him by Peter and nodded.

"Well, old friend. Although we only knew one another a short time it is as if I knew you a lifetime. The words of wisdom you imparted will be with me forever. The Russian toasts and the food. The people you introduced me to and who still miss you. We all miss you, and if there was any way to have you with us, I would make it happen."

Patting the top of the headstone, he continued, "I promised I would take care of your *Zvezda Moya,* and it has taken care of me, instead. With the gold nuggets I found, there will be no worry about making a profit for years to come. Kimalu and his brothers, their families will always have a place to return to and from which to make a living if the seals ever stay away from the coastline again."

Peering around, he saw the empty cemetery. Empty of live people anyway and knew this was the end. He wouldn't have any reason to return. He had thanked his friend in his lifetime and the older man knew how much giving the trading post to Matthew would mean to him. And he hoped he had done with it as the old man had wanted him to. Now, he could continue with the rest of this quest. Finish the trip he needed to take to convince himself he hadn't lost the love of his life. That she was as committed to Matthew as he felt she was.

Once Matthew finished his visit to the graves, he took another public coach across the country toward

Europe. He saw farms and pastures and small villages with wide-open farmland between. It seemed wild and untamed, and he could see why Alaska was such a draw for these people. If they had conquered this land, they could conquer anywhere.

He recognized the name of a small town as being where Tedero had been born. Where his friend moved from once he married his Anna. At one time, it had been a place where sheep and wool had been productive. Tedero explained how the soil had gotten a fungus and all green plants eventually died bringing an end to the grazing. That was when Tedero moved to Alaska, after his Anna had died. The last reason for his remaining in Russia and the reason he needed to leave. Leave his heartache behind and follow friends to the new, rich land across the sea.

The town didn't appear to be any more prosperous after so many years. Old men sat around the taverns drinking and telling stories or playing the marble game Tedero was so fond of playing. Matthew planned on staying there overnight before heading northeast. To see where Tedero lived when he was Matthew's age.

As he tried to clear his mind to sleep, Matthew kept seeing the town as it is and knew his friend would wish it to be different. To be healthy again. To be home for young families. Give work to the young men and women who now left seeking a better life. The town was dying, and Matthew knew Tedero would be crying for its loss.

In the morning, Matthew walked through the buildings where the harvested wool and the thread made by the locals had waited to be exported to cities where it would be woven into cloth and sewn into clothes. But it had all begun in this little town.

Now the buildings had missing window glazing, allowing birds to nest on the interior beams and every niche and cranny. Droppings stained the walls beneath every windowsill. The door was on its last hinge as he went from one large space to another. The damp was everywhere indicating the lack of use, but Matthew thought he could still smell the lanolin left by years of wool storage.

All Matthew could see was the waste. Waste of a building built strong enough to keep the rain and snow out. A waste of workforce getting older without a means of earning a living. An entire village dying year by year as the young move out and the old passed away.

He returned to the tavern where he had spent the night before in an upstairs room. Ordering a vodka, he watched the men play chess and the marble game Tedero was so engrossed in each evening when not playing cards. When an older man noticed his interest, he offered Matthew his place across from his opponent. Matthew smiled and chuckled saying in what Russian he could manage that the game had escaped his ability. Tried to explain how Tedero would laugh at his weak attempts to win.

The men asked about this Tedero and admitted they knew of him or his family who were all deceased now. Their old farm crumbled into disuse. Hearing that, Matthew felt a loss as if hearing his own family ranch had been destroyed.

Another two men joined the talk, and one opened a lovely inlaid board and began laying the marbles out in a pattern. The intricate workmanship appealed to Matthew's artistic nature. He asked if he could see it closer and made sure the man knew Matthew appreciated the time and artistry that had gone into the piece.

With that said, the tavern owner went into the back room and returned with another board with the same sort of inlay work and a chessboard with carving along the edge and containing a drawer which held the chess pieces also finely carved. The man explained one of his six sons had carved both game boards. Matthew asked if his son did anything larger, like tables.

The man indicated through another who spoke some German that all six sons were good with their hands, and they had made some chests to hold their sisters' bridal gifts. Matthew was forming an idea as he noted the large trees that had grown up around the town when the fields could no longer be used for grazing.

"Tell the others I would be interested in buying these game boards in quantity. How much would it cost for one? I will pay for the shipping, but I think many would be interested in these boards back in Alaska. The Russians who remained in Alaska are becoming more affluent and would pay for something like this made in their homeland. Furniture as well if you think the men have the skill to make it."

After hearing Matthew's words explained to them, the men all became quite animated with talk and hand gesturing. They all seemed to have something to say about what could be made and the quality. The tavern owner waved Matthew toward the backrooms. Matthew followed the man and was introduced to his wife before being shown several chests and trunks all carved and painted with designs. Then he was taken to stand before a breakfront with its doors carved picturing a brace of quail and a dead hare dangling from a tree branch. The motif was carried over the front of the entire cabinet, so that from a distance, it represented the story of a successful hunt. The bounty of the lands surrounded by root vegetables and corn.

Matthew was excited. "Your sons made these?"

"Da, da," the older man nodded and continued in too rapid of Russian for Matthew to follow.

"If we can get enough wood just like they used in this piece, I will take all you can make. Tables and chairs, too. Use a dark stain just like they did here." Matthew rubbed his hand over the carvings and felt the fur of the hare and the feathers of the birds. These men had a talent Matthew could appreciate and he knew others would as well. Especially the people of Alaska with their hunger for the nice things they left behind or could finally afford.

In that moment, Matthew knew he would set aside his own gratification of rejoining Katarina and instead help Tedero's hometown survive. It would give the area a new industry which should continue to be needed. They could order wood from anywhere, and the buildings already there could be put into usable condition easily enough. Matthew would buy them and donate them to the town for the furniture makers' use. When there was enough made, he would have it shipped to Alaska. Possibly not Sitka, but there were towns starting all over the territory. Towns occupied by men and women who had made their fortune and who now wanted to enjoy what that fortune could buy. He would send a wire and ask Peter Kashevaroff to buy or rent a warehouse to store the furniture when it arrives and perhaps a store run by one of his family members to sell the items. He could trust Peter to make the right choices. And Peter would appreciate the thoughts behind helping Tedero's hometown.

Overnight the town seemed to have sprouted more people. They showed up to work on getting the large warehouse building cleaned and readied for occupancy. Glass appeared and was cut to fit the empty windowpanes. Walls washed and then painted. Men brought tools and a steam engine was added to run the wood milling side. Evidently it had been decided by the men that trees would arrive whole and sliced into boards before being sanded for use.

Two men who made cabinets would handle making the boards for the cabinet part of the breakfronts and tables, while different woods, softer woods, would be carved into the doors and spindles as needed.

Matthew had drawn different spindle and chairback designs he knew worked. He even drew up a highchair pattern. He felt mirror and photograph frames would be popular as well. Several women showed him examples of their painting skills which he agreed could be used on chairbacks as well as hope chests. He couldn't believe how much talent resided in this town. How much time had been wasted due to lack of finance to set up another industry after sheepherding failed.

The tavern owner accepted the position of managing the furniture-making process. He had gotten all his children involved from the beginning and was already familiar with keeping records and inventory. The man's children were hard workers and talented artisans. Matthew knew this town's furniture would make its mark in Alaska, and soon, special orders would be coming in.

Everywhere Matthew looked, Tedero's hometown was bustling. A livery had started up again to help bring in supplies and take finished products to the southern ports. Taking the same route Matthew had taken to get there. A boardinghouse for the new workers needed was started, also. A shop selling boots and shoes reopened with all the workers needing footwear and having a paycheck to pay for them. And everyone seemed to have a smile and good word for each other when passing one another in the streets. Matthew could see how much happier everyone was and he hoped what he had accomplished in these few weeks would please his old friend, Tedero.

After making sure everyone knew how to get in touch with Peter, Matthew felt he could continue to find his own happiness without guilt. He had used what Tedero had given him to make all those in his hometown happier and productive.

Now everything focused on reaching St. Petersburg. He hadn't taken time to spend any money on dressing himself as a rich man, nor did he travel like a rich man. No sense drawing attention to himself in a poor country.

He spoke with the people on the coach travelling alongside him, tried to converse with the men who steered the ferry, sought any information about the Petrovna family or their holdings. He would check them out in case Boris and Katarina were there or nearby. Each time he was disappointed, it instilled more energy to keep on searching for her. He would begin in earnest in St. Petersburg. Katarina knew that he would do so, and hopefully, she had left him her direction with someone at their home. He had no return letters, but he wouldn't take that as a message she had no interest. He would need to hear it from her lips. Her words tearing his heart to pieces.

Reaching the city added more than half a month to his travels. His first stop was to the Russian bank he was familiar with in Alaska, handed them the letter of credit from Alaska's equivalent, and the letter of introduction from Peter Kashevaroff, which held much sway with the man behind the desk. In fact, the man couldn't offer him Russian tea quickly enough. He went from distrusted foreigner to honored guest.

The bank manager recommended a hotel which recommended an excellent tailor. Matthew found himself dressed as a European with exquisite taste in a matter of days. Now he felt he could face Katarina's father and hold his own. Explain that he loved Katarina and if she was still willing, wished to marry him, he would be more than honored. If that didn't work, he would kidnap her and hide her away until she remembered she loved him.

Thank God, it didn't lead to that. He approached the Patrovka's house, which was in the best area of town, gave the butler his card, which he had been told he needed printed as all wealthy men did, and was shown to a small parlor to wait. He tried not to be intimidated by the heavily carved furniture covered with gold gilt or the impressively large mirrors hanging on every wall along with oil paintings he was sure were painted by master artists. It was an elaborate copy of a European castle, but with a taste of the Far East. He recognized the red enameled chests and ceramic Fu dogs protecting the door the butler went through as being from Asia.

What if, at this very moment, they were securing Katarina away? Taking her someplace he couldn't find her? What if her father never told her Matthew had come to see her, come for her to be his wife? He moved toward the door just as it blew open and a whirlwind he recognized threw itself into his arms.

"Matthew, my Matthew, why did you take so long? I've been so unhappy. I thought you forgot about me. I thought you didn't care, but Papa told me to be patient. That you would come." She buried her head into his shoulder while he held tightly onto her.

She not only had waited, but she was as anxious for them to be together as he was. And what had she said about her father? Was the man actually supporting Matthew's claim to Katarina? And why would Boris tell her anything? Matthew was sure the man hated him and would be livid if he knew what he'd done to his little girl once they were alone in the trading post.

Finally, they felt confident enough in one another to step apart. As if on cue, Boris came in big as a bear, but now wearing a traditional Russian coat over a waistcoat, white shirt, and lace-trimmed cravat, with suede breeches tucked into high glossy boots. He looked as if he wanted to thrash Matthew, but instead gave him a bear hug and slapped him firmly on his back. Matthew retained his footing but barely.

"Well, you said you'd come for my Katarina and now you are here. I always say Alaska is the land where opportunity knows no bounds. Achievement is available to all who are willing to put in the work. I hear of your success and knew you would be coming. Where are the bear teeth? I want to see how big they are."

Matthew wasn't going to look a gift horse in the mouth and accepted the man's hand as it came out to shake his. "I wanted to come sooner, but I had loose ends to tie up. I wanted to ask you for Katarina's hand in person. I wanted to look you in the eyes and promise I'll always take care of her, I'll love her forever, and she'll never want for anything her entire life."

"Well said, Matthew, but what about me?" the big Russian said, seriously with his hands clasped behind his back.

"I don't understand? Do you mean a dowry or something like that?"

"Matthew, a dowry is something the bride brings to the marriage. Papa is speaking of the bride price. He is expecting an offer of horses for my hand. He thinks to be funny."

"If it means I get to marry you, I'll give him a whole herd of Nebraska mustangs."

"No, he wants Przewalski horses from the Mongolian plains. He knows they are difficult for you to get, so he is trying to put barriers in your way." She sent a disapproving look to her father as she explained.

Matthew turned; his brows drawn down. "I thought you approved of me now that I have money."

"Peter Kashevaroff is a friend, and he has been keeping me aware of what you are doing." He held up a big paw. "Nothing he should not have told me. He knew I was interested in you, but not why, although he might have changed his mind knowing you wanted to name the mine after Katarina."

"But I didn't in the end. They were named in honor of my good friend, my first friend in Alaska. I would never be able to sell a mine named after my wife."

"I know that, also. You must remember, I have connections all over the world, but most in the land once owned by Russia. I am mostly interested in where you plan to live with my little Katarina. I am an old man and do not wish her too far away."

Matthew began to understand. Boris wasn't against him or his marrying Katarina but was fearful he would lose his daughter when she married. "I will always consider Nebraska home, but I left because I wanted to see more of the world. As long as I can visit every year or two, then I'd be happy anywhere Katarina is." He pulled her closer and brought his arm around her waist. She gazed up at him, promising him things with her eyes.

"Then, Katarina, if you think you want this American, this Alaskan, I will grant you permission to marry. And grant an old man his wish that you will not be from my side longer than two years. That I will have ample time to see you and my grandchildren until I leave this earth."

She moved into her father's arms, tears in their eyes as she nodded into his chest. "I will, Papa. No one has a better Papa, and I would think it most important to have my children know you as I do."

"Da, that is good. Will I be able to talk you into staying in St. Petersburg after the wedding?"

"I've been gone from home a long time. My brothers are growing up and some of them wanted to go to college. I want to go home and make that happen for them, meet my niece and have them all meet Katarina. They're gonna love her as much as I do. She'll always have a family in Nebraska that way."

"It will be all right, Papa. I will give birth to my

first child here in St. Petersburg and he will have a good strong Russian name."

That promise seemed to do the trick. Boris grinned and began calling out to servants who jumped to do his bidding. Matthew stayed with Katarina on the sofa talking about more of what they will do and places they would go once they were man and wife.

A tap on his door had Matthew smiling widely and then controlled his happiness in case it was Boris there to make sure he hadn't taken a nocturnal walk to Katarina's room which, of course, had crossed his mind. Then he remembered he was in a foreign country with a very protective father in the room somewhere down the hall. It would just have been his luck to knock on a door and have it been Boris's sleeping chamber.

Opening it cautiously, Katarina pushed her way through and then leaned against it as it closed. "I couldn't wait until everyone else was asleep. I needed you so much..."

He leaned into her taking her lips in his own. After feasting for a few minutes, he pushed himself away. "Your father would not approve of this, I'm sure. We need to wait for the priest if I understood everything correctly."

"Yes, but that is for the actual wedding. We can have the wedding night anytime we wish." She practically attacked him, and they found themselves on his open bed with Katarina taking the lead in untying his cravat and tearing at his vest.

"Wait. Wait. Wait, Katarina," he said trying to keep her hands from doing any more damage to his clothing and baring more of his skin to her. He wasn't sure where this chivalry was coming from, but it was there, and he had to acknowledge he felt some guilt for sleeping with her before. Before they were even engaged. "What would your father do if he came through that door right now? What would he think?"

Pushing herself up by her arms, she stared into his eyes making her pelvis grind into his erection in a most satisfying way. "He wouldn't be surprised. If he were, it would only be if I wasn't here with you like this. I am his daughter, and we Russians are very passionate. Didn't I explain that to you in Alaska?"

Grinning he nodded, "Yeah, I kinda remember something like that. Are you sure though? I mean what if you change your mind after being with me again? What if the magic has worn off?"

"You mean what if I no longer love you?"

"Yeah, I guess." He didn't want to hear about her doubts or worries they wouldn't make it as a couple. He didn't want her to think about how different they were and how far apart their lives have been up to now. He didn't want her to think at all, but to feel. Feel his love and feel how they could conquer everything together. Go further than either of them could go alone.

Shaking her head sadly, she whispered, "I never doubted you would come for me. I was ready to wait years if that is what it took, but I knew I did not have the patience, and I had already begun planning my trip back to you. Papa would have made it happen if I had begged enough so I knew we would not be away from one another too much longer. Only you beat me to the punch, as you American's say."

That's all he needed to hear. He rolled her under him and pressed against her clothing which he realized was a thin sleeping gown and robe. Pulling the ties that

149

held the front together he freed her breasts for his lips.

Moving to accommodate his seeking mouth, she sighed contentedly as if this had been something she had craved for months. She felt the same as last time. She tasted the same as last time. And she smelled the same as last time—an essence so much her own he buried his face into the soft skin under her breasts.

"Make love to me, Matthew. I have waited so long for you to come for me..."

"And I have waited so long for you..." He removed the rest of his clothing and pulled her half-naked body under the covers with him. "Now we will make love in Russia and see if it is any different here."

"It couldn't be better, or it may kill me, Matthew. I so want you inside me and make me feel like you did between the furs." She kissed his mouth and pressed up to urge him into motion. Urge hm to begin the journey they would make together.

"I understand, and I agree wholeheartedly, my love, l*yuboy moya*."

Giggling she asked, "Who taught you those words?"

"Without embarrassment, I asked Cumshewa how to say 'my love' in Russian. He never asked why I wanted to know. I have a pretty advanced vocabulary if I do say so myself."

Still chuckling, she asked, "Are we going to have a language lesson or make love?"

Positioning himself, he assured her, "We are definitely going to make love. I lose my mind when we're together."

"Then let us lose our minds, my darling, because I think we have both waited long enough. Let the world pass us by if it must, but you and I will be as one as we were meant to be."

CHAPTER TWELVE

"I have always been a good traveler, especially at sea. Maybe it was something I ate that doesn't agree with me?" Katarina took a small sip of water to rinse her mouth.

Wiping her face with a cool cloth, Matthew tucked strands of her hair behind her ear. She looked as green as some of those men he travelled with to Sitka over a year ago. "I'll get you some tea. I know, I know, Russian tea." He assured her as he went to summon the steward. "I could order something light to eat if you think you can keep it down."

Smiling, she shook her head. "I feel much better already. It must have been something I ate." She stood up and slammed the cover down on the convenience located in the small room off their stateroom.

"We rushed around the past couple of weeks preparing for this trip. Perhaps it's all the excitement." He offered in way of an excuse trying not to worry any more about her malaise than she apparently did.

"Perhaps it is all the lovemaking my husband insists upon." She brushed the front of his trousers and had his immediate attention.

"Don't start anything you can't finish, Mrs. Foster. I'm not a man to be trifled with."

"This 'trifled'? It is a good thing?"

Chuckling, he pulled her onto the bed whispering,

"A very good thing. Do you really need that tea?"

"No, as I said, I feel quite all right now, but you can show me how you planned to alleviate my distress if you wish."

"Oh, I more than wish. Come here, wife." He began by kissing her and moved to a favorite spot beneath her ear where he sucked for a minute before opening her robe and taking a delectable nipple into the warmth of his mouth. God, he loved this woman. How would he live if she were really ill? What could he do to make sure she was never less than safe and happy?

They made love. She was as responsive as always perhaps even more so. He sent his seed deeply into her as she convulsed around him, and they slept for another hour, missing breakfast and the Russian tea.

"I don't feel well again. Oh, Matthew, I feel hot and ill…"

He worriedly thought about Lorelei when she was bitten by the poisonous snake and her fever spiked. They were all so frightened she would die. Die while carrying Luke's baby. Baby!

"I think I know why you're not feeling well, darling. I think you're with child. I mean I can't be sure, but it's been weeks now and…"

"…and I haven't had my courses. Oh, Matthew, I think you are right. I think I'm going to have a baby."

Pulling her into his arms, he held her tightly. "Then it's as well we took this trip now. We can stay the two months or so as planned in America and then be back to St. Petersburg in plenty of time as we promised. This child will be born in Russia, have a Russian name, and a grandfather that will spoil it as badly as he did his own child."

"Oh, Matthew, you were doing so well, and then you had to spoil it."

"Tell me I'm wrong."

She smiled and kissed him instead, batting her lashes at him as she looked up through them. "I love you, Mr. Foster."

"And I love you, Mrs. Foster, wife and soon-to-be mother of my child." He covered her hand as it lay over her stomach. This was such a wonderful end to his Alaskan adventure. He would have quite a tale to tell Lorelei and his brothers once they reached Nebraska.

A word about the author...

I have been reading as far back as I can remember. After years of reading other authors' work, I decided to let my imaginary people have their say.

www.authorsusanpayne.com